A SOFT PLACE
TO FALL

Other books by Betsy Rogers:

The Healing Heart
Rescued Hearts

A SOFT PLACE TO FALL

•

Betsy Rogers

AVALON BOOKS
NEW YORK

Published by Avalon Books,
an imprint of Thomas Bouregy & Co., Inc.
160 Madison Avenue, New York, NY 10016

Library of Congress Cataloging-in-Publication Data

Rogers, Betsy.
  A soft place to fall / Betsy Rogers.
        p.   cm.
  ISBN 978-0-8034-7669-1 (acid-free paper)
  1. Biological stations—Peru—Fiction.   2. Americans—
Peru—Fiction.   3. Biologists—Fiction.   4. Rain forests—
Peru—Fiction.   I. Title.
  PS3568.O3955S64 2011
  813'.54—dc22

                                        2011005556

PRINTED IN THE UNITED STATES OF AMERICA
ON ACID-FREE PAPER
BY RR DONNELLEY, BLOOMSBURG, PENNSYLVANIA

Chapter One

Julie Winlock was lost in the Peruvian rain forest.

An hour earlier, she had stepped off the dirt path to sketch an orchid with white petals streaked with gold. Then she had spotted an even more exotic orchid a few yards beyond that one and had walked over to it for a closer look.

As she sketched that flower, a crimson beauty with pouting "lips," a butterfly with iridescent-blue wings flitted from blossom to blossom. Julie paused in her sketching to gaze at it. It was one of the most beautiful creatures she had ever laid eyes on.

Finally, the butterfly floated up and up, disappearing into the dense forest canopy high above Julie's head.

Julie studied her drawing for a moment before closing her sketching pad. She put the pad and her colored pencils into her cloth shoulder bag. Then, confident that she knew the way back, she turned around and began retracing her steps to the path.

Or so she thought.

Several minutes went by as Julie threaded her way through

the foliage. She stopped and looked around with a puzzled air. She should have reached the path by that time.

"I know it's here somewhere," she muttered under her breath. "Come on, path, where are you?"

She headed off in a different direction, thinking she'd spotted an opening. But when she got there, she found that the opening was not the route back to the Manu River Research Station. It was merely an empty space where a large tree had once stood.

Julie stepped around the fallen giant, which was draped with tropical vines and air plants, and thought for a moment. She hadn't passed this downed tree before. She was sure of it.

Julie took a deep breath. *I'm not lost,* she told herself. *Not lost. Just a little turned around, that's all.*

But as she scanned her surroundings, a flutter of apprehension stirred in her stomach. In the muted, greenish light of the rain forest, everything looked the same. In such an unfamiliar setting, Julie's normally good sense of direction had failed her. For all she knew, she was walking *away* from the path, instead of *toward* it.

She took another calming breath and gathered her wits. Maybe she ought to go back to the place where she had taken her first wrong turn. She remembered a tree stump at that spot, one with mushrooms growing on top of it. Finding that stump should be easy, she reasoned. From there, surely she could locate the path.

Ten minutes later, Julie arrived at a marshy area. Small creeks ran this way and that. Pools shimmered among the trees, and the ground was soft and wet beneath her feet.

Julie stopped in dismayed confusion as water oozed around her shoes. She knew she hadn't crossed any creeks on her way into the forest. Once again, she had traveled in the wrong direction and had no idea where she was.

Julie retreated to dry ground. She felt a lump of panic rise in her throat. She fought the urge to plunge off in a new direction, running to save time. She knew that such reckless behavior might take her even deeper into the trackless jungle of the eastern Andes. The thought filled her with dread.

As hard as it was to accept, Julie admitted to herself that she was lost.

Really lost.

And now she had to pull her act together and make smart decisions. She wracked her brain. What were the two basic rules for survival in such a situation?

First, she must remain calm. And, second, she must stop moving around and stay where she was. With any luck, someone from the research station would come looking for her.

But how long will that take? she wondered. *The sun will set in an hour or so.* Julie dreaded the thought of having to spend an unscheduled night in a tropical rain forest.

But she might have to.

She made a quick survey of her clothing and gear, mentally preparing herself for that possibility. She was wearing light trousers and a tank top. Her bag contained a half-empty bottle of water, a candy bar, and an orange. She also had a small umbrella, a flashlight, and a bandanna. It wasn't much, but it would have to do.

Julie moistened her lips and faced reality. Many long, uncomfortable hours stretched before her unless someone found her soon. She shivered as she imagined being alone after dark in such an unfamiliar environment. Visions of biting insects and prowling nocturnal animals flickered through her mind, fueling her anxiety.

And, if it rained during the night, which seemed likely—she was lost in a *rain* forest, after all—she'd only have her small umbrella for protection from the downpour. Damp and miserable, hungry and afraid, she'd count herself lucky to survive such an ordeal.

"What an idiot!" she said, scolding herself out loud. If only she hadn't left the path to sketch those orchids! She'd know better next time.

If she *got* a next time, that is.

At the very least, Julie would have some explaining to do. She'd arrived by boat at the Manu River Research Station that afternoon, hoping to make a good first impression on Doctor Maxwell Stuart.

Doctor Stuart, from the United States, was the wildlife biologist who ran the station. Julie was looking forward to meeting him. But she was nervous too, having been warned that the biologist would not be pleased over the reason for Julie's visit. She knew she had a tough sell ahead of her.

Except for the cook, a friendly Peruvian gentleman named Hernando, the research station had been deserted when Julie arrived. In broken English, Hernando had explained that Doctor Stuart and the others were out in the field and would be back before dinner.

Julie had spent her entire life, all twenty-nine years of it, in Seattle, Washington. She'd never been to a tropical rain forest before, and she was brimming with excitement. While waiting to meet Doctor Stuart, her natural curiosity had led her down a beckoning path. She'd only meant to be gone for a few minutes, and she hadn't intended to walk very far. Now she regretted having given in to her urge to explore, an impulse that had landed her in her present predicament.

Julie swatted at a mosquito and adjusted her shoulder bag. She looked around at the confusing green maze of dappled light and tangled vines and shook her head with chagrin. Her first day at the research station and she was already lost. What would Doctor Stuart think of her?

"So much for making a good impression," she muttered.

Julie might be lost, but she wasn't going to simply stand there and do nothing. She cupped her hands around her mouth and began yelling for help.

"Hello! Can anyone hear me?"

Several minutes ticked by in the hot, humid jungle. Julie called again and again, hoping that someone would hear her shouts and come to get her.

But no human voice answered back. The only sounds reaching Julie's ears were those of frogs croaking in the water and of eerie birdcalls filtering through the trees.

Julie tried again.

"Hello! Hello!"

She paused to listen. The noise of a snapping twig made her jump, her nerves on edge. Something tickled her ankle. She lifted the cuff of her trousers and found ants crawling over her bare skin. She brushed them off and danced to one side.

More time passed and Julie's discomfort intensified. Her mouth and throat felt dry, as her sense of foreboding increased. A trickle of sweat ran down her neck, and then continued its path to the hollow between her breasts. Her heavy, shoulder-length hair clung to the back of her neck, making her feel even warmer in the steamy climate.

She searched her pockets for a rubber band. Finding none, Julie improvised. She pulled a strip of woody fiber from a vine and used it to tie her chestnut hair on top of her head. Then she pulled out her cotton bandanna, covered her hair, and knotted the bandanna at the nape of her neck.

"Oh, that's better," she murmured, and began fanning herself with a big leaf.

A mosquito landed on her wrist and bit her. She slapped at the insect. More mosquitoes swarmed around her face.

"Get away from me!" she said, flailing her arms.

Just then, Julie thought she heard something. She froze in place and held her breath, straining her ears to listen. Was it her imagination, or had the sound of a man's voice just drifted through the trees?

The shout came again. This time there could be no doubt. Someone with a deep, masculine voice was calling in the forest.

"Hello," the man yelled, sounding closer. "Can you hear me?"

"Yes," said Julie, shouting back, "but I can't see you. I'm over here." Then she added, "I'm—I'm sort of lost."

"Yeah, I already figured that out," said the man, with a short, rumbling laugh. "That's why I've come looking for you."

"Thank goodness," she called, with a surge of relief.

Julie glanced this way and that, trying to penetrate the walls of green with her eyes. But she still couldn't see her rescuer.

"My name's Julie Winlock," she said. "Who are you?"

"I'm Maxwell Stuart."

Oh no, thought Julie, with a sinking feeling. The boss himself had come searching for her. *How embarrassing.* She couldn't think of a more awkward way of meeting Doctor Stuart for the first time.

He sounded much younger than she'd expected, in his early thirties perhaps. Julie tried to conjure a mental picture of the man, going on the rich timbre of his voice alone. He sounded self-confident, in charge, and very attractive.

He called again. "Julie?"

"Yes."

"I'm on the path," he said. "Just walk in the direction of my voice and you'll be okay."

"Uh, well—" Julie hesitated.

"What is it?"

"Do you mean through the swamp?"

"What swamp?"

"The one that's between here and where you are," said Julie. "I'm standing at the edge of a big swampy area."

"Don't worry about it," said Doctor Stuart, with a hint of impatience. "Come on, it'll be dark soon. I have a flashlight, but I'd rather get you out of here before nightfall. Now, just walk toward my voice." He stopped. "You *are* wearing boots, aren't you?"

"Not really," said Julie, glancing down at her feet.

"Not really?" he said. "Well, what *do* you have on?"

"Walking shoes."

"You mean, with low tops?"

"Yes."

Julie heard him mutter something unintelligible. Although she couldn't make out the words, the tone was clear enough. She'd been careless and gotten herself lost. Now she was being uncooperative, a real pain in the neck. Well, Julie admitted to herself, if that was Doctor Stuart's opinion of her, she honestly couldn't blame him.

His voice broke in on her thoughts.

"Okay, new plan," he said, blowing out his breath. "Just stay where you are. I'm coming in there to get you."

Julie bit her lip. Things were going from bad to worse. She had to do something.

"Doctor Stuart?"

"What?" he said, like a man trying to mask his irritation.

"I'm sorry for all the trouble," she said.

"Never mind," he said, "we can talk about it later."

"You know," said Julie, getting an idea, "I think I can make it on my own. The water doesn't look very deep. So what if I get my feet wet. It's no big deal."

"Getting your feet wet is not the issue," he said.

"Well, then—"

"Snakes," he barked. "The issue is snakes, poisonous snakes that love water."

"Oh, I see," she said, in a small voice. She cast a nervous glance around, half expecting to find a serpent with its fangs exposed swimming in her direction.

"I can't let you walk through there on your own," he said. "Not without boots. Now do as I tell you. Stay put, and talk me toward you. I'm on my way."

A few minutes later, the splashing sounds of someone wading through water reached Julie's ears.

"Over here," she called, guiding Doctor Stuart toward her. "Keep coming this way."

Julie scanned the green filigree of forest, willing him to appear. Presently, some motion beneath the trees caught her eye. She focused on the spot and saw the brief outline of a man moving in her direction. The man disappeared behind some foliage, and the sounds of splashing stopped. A deep voice came from among the trees.

"Julie?"

"I'm over here," she said, cupping her hands around her mouth. "You're on the right track. Just keep coming."

A few minutes later, Doctor Stuart materialized from the forest. Wading in knee-deep water, he covered the last few yards of the pool nearest Julie and joined her on dry land.

"Am I ever glad to see you," said Julie, smiling in gratitude. She gave a nervous laugh as she looked up into his cobalt-blue eyes. "My hero," she added, trying to use a touch of humor to lighten the situation. "Thanks for coming out to rescue me, Doctor Stuart."

"Well, I'm no hero," he said, with a note of gruff irony. He tipped his head at her. "But you're welcome."

Julie studied him for a moment. If she'd expected the wild-life biologist to be a stuffy, professorial type with horn-rimmed glasses and a pith helmet, she was enjoying a most pleasant surprise.

Doctor Maxwell Stuart was a big hunk of a man, well over six feet tall, and he radiated good health and vigor. He was wearing khaki jungle pants, a blue shirt with long sleeves, and a well-worn photographer's vest with many pockets. Rubber waders sheathed his legs to mid-thigh level, giving him the dashing look of a buccaneer.

His head was bare, and his hair was thick and dark. His features and the handsome shape of his head made Julie think of Hugh Jackman, with a playful dash of George Clooney around the eyes and mouth. A velvet paw of animal attraction curled in her stomach.

"Thanks again," she said, letting out her breath.

"Don't mention it," he said. Then he added, "I just have one question before we start back." He fixed her with his impossibly blue eyes and hooked a thumb over his shoulder. "What in the world are you doing out here?"

"I was just looking around," said Julie, with a self-conscious shrug.

"But you left the path," he said, with an accusing frown. "That's a big no-no in the rain forest."

"I saw some beautiful orchids," said Julie. "And, I . . . well, I walked over to sketch them. Here, let me show you."

She fumbled in her shoulder bag and brought out her sketching pad. She flipped it open to her drawing of the crimson orchid.

He looked at the drawing and his expression changed.

"Hmm, not bad," he said, admiring her work.

"I also saw a beautiful blue butterfly," she said, remembering the scene. "I'd never seen one like it before. It had the most amazing iridescent wings."

"If you like butterflies," he said, "you've come to the right place. There're over twelve hundred species of butterfly in this part of Peru."

"Wow," said Julie, noting the spark of enthusiasm in his eyes. "That's really impressive."

"Well, we're in Manu National Park, after all," he reminded her. "This is one of the most biodiverse places on earth."

She nodded.

"The butterfly you saw," he continued, "was probably one of the blue morphos. It's a common genus. You'll see a lot of them here."

He nodded toward her drawing.

"That's a common genus of orchid too," he said. He regarded her from beneath lowered brows. "Trust me, you don't need to leave the path to find those."

"But it was the first one I'd ever seen," said Julie, tucking the sketching pad back into her bag. "I just had to draw it."

"Yeah," he admitted, gazing down at her, "there's something special about the first one. I know what you mean."

"I only stepped a few yards off the path," said Julie. "I was sure I could find my way back, but somehow I got turned around." She gestured toward the leafy walls of green that encircled them. "It's a little confusing out here, isn't it?"

"Yes, everything looks the same," he said, "which is why you never, ever leave the path without marking the way back. That," he added, raising his forefinger, "is rule number one around here."

"I'll remember that," she said, nodding.

"And while we're on the subject of rules," he said, "I can't believe what you're wearing."

His eyes swept over Julie's body, a quick scan from head to toe. His gaze lingered for a second or two at the base of her throat before returning to her face.

Julie felt a flush warm her cheeks at such frank assessment.

"What do you mean?" she said, feeling exposed.

"The pants are okay, but look at that skimpy little thing you've got on top," he said, mildly scolding her.

Julie glanced down at her bare shoulders and arms.

"With all of that naked skin," he continued, "you're a walking lunch counter for insects. The only thing missing is a big neon sign over your head that says BITE ME."

In spite of herself, Julie giggled at his colorful imagery.

"Hey, I'm not joking," he said, chiding her. "This is serious, Julie. You're in the rain forest and you need to dress appropriately. You can wear whatever you like around camp, but when you're out here, you need to cover up as much skin as possible. I'm talking about long-sleeved shirts as well as long pants. Got it?"

"But it's so hot," said Julie, tasting salty beads of moisture on her upper lip.

Just then, as if on cue, a mosquito landed on Julie's shoulder.

Before she could react, Doctor Stuart reached out to gently brush it away.

As his fingers grazed her skin, his hand momentarily cupping the curve of her arm, Julie realized, with a jolt of yearning, how much she missed a man's touch. Once again, she felt a tremor of attraction pass through her.

"See what I mean about insects?" he said.

"Yes, I do," said Julie, fanning another mosquito away from her face. "From now on, long pants and long sleeves."

"Fine," he said, "and ditch those shoes. Did you bring any boots with you?"

"Not like those," she said, indicating his thigh-high waders. "Is that what I'm supposed to wear out here?"

"No," he said, "I just happen to have these on because I was out on the river all day. Normally, I wear regular hiking boots."

"Oh," said Julie, "I brought some of those."

"Good," he said. "Wear them."

Julie took a deep breath. She felt as if she were an erring child that had been sent to the principal's office for a scolding. But she knew that Doctor Stuart was only trying to look out for her safety.

"I promise to wear my boots, Doctor Stuart," she said, and smiled at him.

He acknowledged her pledge with a little nod. "You know, we're pretty informal around here," he said, his tone softening a bit. "Call me Max."

"All right, Max," said Julie, extending her hand. "Happy to meet you."

He grasped her hand with his warm fingers and palm, his firm flesh pressing into hers. Julie's hand almost disappeared in his grip, one that was both strong and, she sensed, capable of the gentlest of caresses. She withdrew from the physical contact feeling a bit flustered, her emotions in a whirl.

Max glanced around at the gathering gloom. "Let's head back," he said. "As I mentioned, I have a flashlight with me, but it'll be easier if we don't have to use it." He looked at Julie. "Do you happen to have a flashlight in that bag of yours?"

"Yes, I do."

"Good," he said. Then he added, "Still, a flashlight and a sketching pad aren't exactly a full survival kit. It's a good thing you won't have to spend the night out here."

"So I don't have all the right gear with me at the moment," said Julie, damping down a spurt of irritation. "I think we've already established that."

"Yes, we have," he said, in the tone of a lecturing professor, but Julie caught a twinkle in his eye. Max was having sport with her.

"I didn't mean to get lost, you know," said Julie, deciding to match his teasing barb, one for one. "And, if I'd intended to spend the night out here, I would've brought a tent, a sleeping bag, *and* my portable espresso machine for morning coffee." She tilted her head at him, daring him to challenge her. "So there."

Max gave a throaty gust of laughter, a lovely, deep sound filled with mirth and good nature.

"Okay," he said, smiling at her. "Point taken."

"By the way," said Julie, "how did you know where to look for me?"

"Our cook Hernando saw you head down one of the paths," said Max. "There're a lot of trails leading away from the research station, so it was sheer good luck that he saw which one you took. That made it relatively easy to come looking for you. Otherwise, you really would've spent the night out here." He chuckled. "Without your espresso machine."

"Now that's what I call roughing it," said Julie, returning his banter. Yet she knew how potentially serious her situation could've been. "I'll have to thank Hernando when we get back to the research station," she added.

"Speaking of which," said Max, "let's get going."

"What about my shoes?" said Julie, glancing down at her feet. "I distinctly remember you saying something about water-loving snakes."

"That's right," said Max, "which is why I'm going to carry you back to the path."

"Carry me?" said Julie.

"Yep, that's the plan," said Max, tossing her a teasing smile. "How else are you and I going to get back in one piece?"

"I guess I thought we'd both wade back, with you in the lead," said Julie, "and that we'd keep an eye out for snakes."

"Can't take the risk," said Max, shaking his head. "Now, what'll it be? Do you prefer piggyback, sitting on my shoulders, or riding in my arms? It's your call."

Julie quickly weighed her options, eliminating the first two at once. She didn't want to perch on Max's shoulders like a toddler hoisted aloft to watch a parade, and she certainly had no wish to straddle his back like a sack of potatoes.

No contest, thought Julie. She knew what she wanted. She wanted to be carried in Max's arms like a woman, not like a child or a bag of produce.

"In your arms, please," she said, feeling as if she'd just won the lottery.

"Okay," said Max, "let's do it."

He hooked Julie's bag over his shoulder. Then he stepped forward and, with one effortless move, swept Julie off her feet. He tucked her slender form against his chest, one arm cradling her bent knees, the other arm firmly wrapped around her with his hand on her waist.

Max stood there for a second or two, giving Julie a chance to get settled.

"Put your arms around my neck," he instructed. "That's right. Now just hang on and let me do the rest."

He paused and looked into her face, a mere few inches from his own.

"I can feel you tensing up, Julie," he said. He gave her a re-assuring little jiggle. "Try to relax, okay?"

"Yes, okay," said Julie, attempting to calm her pulse rate, which had increased to an excited flutter.

But relaxing in Max's embrace was easier said than done, because lovely, warm sensations were rippling through her like waves stroking a beach. She'd never been held in such strong, masculine arms before, as if she weighed nothing. The feeling was exquisite beyond words.

"Ready?" he said.

"Yes," said Julie, "I'm ready."

"Okay, here we go."

Chapter Two

As Max stepped from dry land and carefully waded into the water, Julie instinctively knew that she was safe in his arms. He would neither lose his grip on her nor falter in any way. Strong and confident, he was capable of carrying Julie across Peru and back, with ease.

Julie's mind suddenly harked back in time, as she recalled her husband Simon. She couldn't help but compare the two men. An inch shorter than Julie, and with a slight, wiry frame, Simon had never carried her. Except, that is, for the one time on their wedding day, when he'd lifted her over the threshold of their new apartment.

Oh, Simon, she thought, with regret. She still couldn't think about him without getting a lump in her throat.

Julie forced her mind back to the present, allowing her senses to take over. Mingling with the cadence of Max's steps through the water was the mellow croaking of frogs and the soft rustling of leaves. A squeak alerted her to a tiny rain forest bat as it flew by, a bundle of velvet on delicate wings.

Julie's sense of touch registered the pleasant contact of the side of her body, from shoulder to hip, pressing against Max's broad chest. His warmth melted into her, and she could feel the beating of his heart. She laced her fingers more securely behind the strong column of his neck, noting the soft brush of his hair on the back of her hands.

"Doing okay?" he asked, adjusting his grip as he checked on her.

"Yes," said Julie, "everything's just fine." *More than fine,* she silently added.

She inhaled a deep breath. Flowers and the primal fragrance of green abundance perfumed the warm air. Max himself gave off an intoxicating brew of scents. Julie detected a clean, soapy smell, as well as an electrifying note that was pure male. She closed her eyes, the better to focus and simply take it all in, every tantalizing molecule.

"You look as if you're enjoying yourself," said Max, his breath fanning her cheek. He spoke softly, as if not to disturb their surroundings. "What's going through your mind?"

"Oh," said Julie, gathering her thoughts, "I was just thinking that this is a Garden of Eden. It's no wonder people rave about the rain forest."

"It's the most lush environment on earth," said Max, "which is why I love it so much. There's nowhere else I'd rather be." He chuckled. "Well, for six months of the year, that is."

"What about the rest of the year?" said Julie, opening her eyes to observe Max's features. Her gaze lingered longest on the appealing curve of his mouth.

"That's when I organize my field notes and write articles for various scientific journals," he said. "I also lead seminars at universities and colleges around the Seattle area. Now and then, I'm asked to speak at a world conference." He paused. "I was in Paris last March."

"Paris in the spring," murmured Julie, musing on the French city of lights and lovers. "I've never been to Paris. Is it as romantic as I've always heard?"

"Oh, it's romantic, all right," said Max with feeling, his voice vibrating near Julie's ear. "Everywhere you look there are couples holding hands or kissing." He gave a short, rueful laugh. "Unfortunately, I was there on my own."

"That must have been a little lonely," said Julie. She imagined Max sitting by himself at a sidewalk café, no doubt attracting admiring glances from every female passerby.

"Lonely?" said Max, his legs making steady progress through the water. "Yes, I guess I was a bit lonely in Paris, now that you mention it. But, hey," he went on, with what sounded like forced optimism, "you can't have it all, right?"

"No, I suppose not," said Julie, thinking about her own recent disappointments. "In any case," she went on, shifting gears, "you certainly do lead an interesting life."

"Well, it has a nice balance," he said, nodding. "I get paid to go off adventuring in the rain forest every six months. Who wouldn't love that?" he added, in an aside. "Then I have the privilege of sharing what I've learned with others. Hopefully, I'm making a difference in the way people view the environment."

He gave a thoughtful pause, seeming to fix his gaze on a far, distant point. Julie saw a flicker of mixed emotions tense the corners of his eyes.

"It's a good life," he concluded.

"Do you live in Seattle?" said Julie, curious to know more about him.

"Oh, no." said Max, shaking his head. "The city's gotten too hectic for me. I live near a small town east of Seattle. I've got a nice, quiet place on thirty acres, where I converted a wonderful old barn into a house."

"That must have been a satisfying project," said Julie. She could easily picture Max astride a barn roof, wearing a leather carpenter's belt slung low on his hip and masterfully wielding a hammer and nails.

"It was actually my wife's idea," said Max. His eyes darkened as he corrected himself. "Former wife, I should say. Ironically, she never lived there, as it turned out."

Again, Julie saw a subtle mix of emotions cross Max's face. Was she detecting sorrow, or bitterness, or maybe a combination of those? She wasn't sure. But what was clear was that an experience in Max's past had taken its toll on him.

That makes two of us, she thought, her heart squeezing.

"So, Max," she said, steering the conversation back to safer ground, "what's your specialty out here?"

She studied his profile and saw the tension drain from his face. He had a well-shaped nose, a strong chin, and a wide, intelligent forehead.

A lock of dark hair had fallen over his brow. Julie felt the temptation to sweep the lock back into place for him. But she stayed her hand, knowing how intimate such a grooming gesture would be, however casual.

Besides, she rather liked the wayward lock of hair right where it was. It gave Max's handsome face a rakish touch, enhancing his image as a jungle explorer.

"My specialty is tropical birds," he said, answering her question. "I also know a lot about rain forest plants and mammals. As the director of the station, I need a working knowledge in all the disciplines." A spark lit up his eyes. "But my first love is birds."

"Hmm."

"What about you?" he said, turning to regard her face. "What are you interested in?"

It suddenly dawned on Julie that Max apparently hadn't made the connection between her and the Pierson-Roth Foundation, the organization that supported the Manu River Research Station. Hadn't he gotten the message that Julie would be paying a call as Pierson-Roth's newly hired representative?

For a moment, Julie considered sharing with Max the purpose of her visit. Then she thought better of it. There'd be plenty of time for that. Why ruin the friendly, easy mood between them by bringing up controversy that could cause bad feelings?

"Oh, I'm interested in everything," she said, with a non-committal shrug. "I'm here to study and learn," she added, which was a truthful statement, if not the complete answer.

"Hmm," said Max, giving a thoughtful nod. "Oh, heads up, here's our first marker."

He stopped beside a low-hanging branch, from which dangled a neon-orange strip of plastic tape.

"As I walked toward the sound of your voice," he said, explaining to Julie, "I tied one of these markers every few yards." He motioned with his head. "There's our next one over there."

Julie looked where Max was indicating. She saw another strip of orange plastic fluttering against the green backdrop of the forest.

"I see it," she said, turning back to him. "The color stands out like a beacon, doesn't it?"

"That's the whole idea," he said. "With these markers, we won't get lost out here. They even show up in the dark, as long as you have a flashlight. All we have to do is follow them and we're home safe."

"Smart idea," said Julie.

"I suggest you file it away for future use," he added, lifting one brow. "I don't want to have to come looking for you again."

"You won't have to," she said, and meant it.

Just then Julie felt a twinge of hunger and fatigue. It had taken her four days to travel to that remote spot on the map. First she'd flown from Seattle to Lima, Peru, and then boarded a train to Cuzco, the ancient capital of the Inca Empire. After spending the night in colorful Cuzco, she'd endured a tooth-rattling ride on a local "chicken bus," up and over the Andes, followed by an all-day journey in a motorized dugout canoe.

Time zones and hard travel were catching up with her. She stifled a yawn as she looked forward to a hot meal and a good night's sleep. She wondered what Hernando, the camp cook, would serve for dinner.

"We're going to untie these markers as we go," said Max. "I don't like to leave strips of plastic in the forest if I don't have to."

"Any special reason?" said Julie, genuinely curious.

"Because they're unsightly," said Max, "and they're not part of the natural scene. They don't belong out here."

"I see."

"Part of my job," he continued, "is to keep this area, this Garden of Eden as you called it, as pristine and uncluttered as possible."

He waded closer to the orange plastic.

"My hands are kind of occupied at the moment," he said, his quick smile telling Julie that he didn't mind the reason for that at all. "So you're going to have to grab that."

As Julie reached for the strip of plastic, leaning out as Max steadied her, her bandanna came loose and started slipping off her head. She caught the bandanna before it could land in the water.

"May I?" she said, asking permission to stuff the cloth into one of Max's vest pockets, which was handier than her bag at the moment.

"Sure," he said.

Julie noticed that Max's eyes were drinking in the sight of her hair, which, to that point, had been concealed.

She put the bandanna into Max's pocket. The task felt easy and familiar, as if she and Max had known each other for years.

Then she reached again for the strip of plastic and untied it from the branch. She gave it a triumphant wave before stuffing it, as well, into Max's vest pocket.

"What a team," she said, smiling as they continued on their way.

"Yes, what a team," he murmured. He cleared his throat and shifted his gaze to the route ahead of them. "Okay, let's get the next one."

Shortly they arrived at the second marker. This time, when Julie stretched out her arm and untied the plastic, the piece of vine loosely holding her hair in place unraveled and fell off. Her heavy chestnut tresses tumbled about her face and shoulders.

"Memo to self," she said, laughing as she watched the vine float away, "never go into the rain forest without a rubber band." She looked at the strip of plastic in her hand. "This would work, I suppose," she added, and prepared to use the strip to tie her hair into a ponytail.

"No, don't," said Max, stopping her.

"I'm sorry?" said Julie, pausing.

"I mean, do as you like," he corrected, with a studied shrug of indifference.

But Julie could tell that Max was not indifferent to what she did with her hair. She'd seen the flicker of admiration in his eyes when the length of vine had come undone and her hair had spilled about her face. She suspected that Max, like a lot of men, preferred a woman's long hair to flow naturally, free and unfettered.

"You know," said Julie, keeping her tone casual, "I think I'll, um, just leave it the way it is. It feels good to let it hang loose for a change."

She shook out her hair and ran her fingers through its length. Some of the flying locks brushed against Max's neck and chest.

"Using a vine to tie back your hair," said Max, with a chuckle. "I've never seen that done before."

Julie smiled with him, enjoying their friendly banter.

Then she felt a shiver of misgiving. The harmonious atmosphere between her and Max would surely disappear when he learned the actual purpose of her visit. She dreaded talking to him about it, but she knew that she couldn't put it off much longer. It was her job, after all.

She wondered how best to broach the subject. Should she flat out tell him in twenty-five words or less exactly why the Pierson-Roth Foundation had sent her there?

Or should she ease into the topic slowly, with the caution of a foreign diplomat?

Hmm. Maybe she'd bring it up after dinner that night when Max would be relaxed and, hopefully, in a receptive frame of mind.

Julie gave an inward sigh of apprehension. However she chose to reveal the nature of her mission, it was sure to be difficult. And, she could already guess how Max would react. She was learning a great deal about the man as they made their way through the swamp. Max loved his work and he loved the rain forest. He was dedicated to its preservation. When he heard what she had to say, he was bound to be angry, upset, and very disappointed. And, Julie admitted to herself, who could fault him? She just hoped that Max wouldn't blame *her* for the changes coming to the research station. The changes were the Foundation's idea, not Julie's. She was just the messenger.

"Here we are," said Max, as they reached dry land.

Julie reluctantly unlaced her fingers from behind Max's neck and slid to the ground. She was sorry to break the physical contact with his chest and strong arms.

She glanced up at Max. She'd felt safe and protected nestled against him, as if nothing could harm her. Such emotions contrasted sharply with how vulnerable she'd felt in the last year. The warm circle of Max's embrace had temporarily erased Julie's fears, but had also reminded her of how much she missed a man's attentions.

"Thanks for the lift," she said, keeping her tone casual as she looked into his eyes. "It was lucky for me that you were wearing waders."

"Yes, wasn't it," he said, slanting a smile at her.

Julie could tell that holding her in his arms had been pleasant for Max as well. The realization sent a flash of heat radiating through her. She felt a powerful attraction to the man, a sizzling chemistry that flowed from him to her and back again. Did Max feel it too?

They walked a short distance through the forest in single file, with Max in the lead. Soon they arrived at the path.

Max untied the last of the plastic strips he'd used as way markers and stuffed it into his pocket. He regarded Julie.

"We're less than a mile from the research station," he said. "It won't take us long to get there."

"Good," said Julie, adjusting her shoulder bag for the walk back. "I'm starving for something besides snacks."

Just then a large butterfly with lustrous wings flew into the open space above the path. It fluttered toward Julie and Max like a scrap of blue borrowed from a summer sky.

"Oh, look, there's another one of those butterflies," said Julie, pointing out the creature before it melted back into the rain forest. "Blue morpho, right?"

Max nodded.

"Now I've seen two of them," said Julie, smiling. "They're incredibly beautiful, aren't they?"

"Yes, they are," said Max. "I see them every day, but I hope I never take them for granted."

"What makes their wings so shiny?" said Julie.

"The iridescence," said Max, "is caused by light reflecting off tiny scales on their wings. I've got some scientific papers on the morpho genus in my office if you're interested."

"Thanks," said Julie.

"One of the studies," continued Max, "has shown that morphos—"

He stopped in mid-sentence and regarded Julie. A puzzled expression crossed his handsome features.

"Wait a minute," he said, tilting his head to one side. He fixed Julie with questioning eyes. "Are you telling me that you've only seen *two* morphos in your life?"

"That's right."

"But how is that possible?"

"What do you mean?"

"Blue morphos," said Max, "are just as common in Costa Rica as they are here."

"I'm sorry?" said Julie, confused. "What are you talking about?"

"I'm talking about morpho butterflies in Costa Rica," said Max, staring at Julie with his thumbs hooked in his back pockets. "You must have seen hundreds of them when you were there doing your postgraduate work."

"I've never been to Costa Rica," said Julie, trying to make sense of the conversation.

"But it says so in the resume you sent to me last fall," said Max, with a little frown. "By the way," he added, in an aside, "I didn't think you'd be here until next Tuesday. You're a week early."

"Oh, you know what?" said Julie, as she finally understood Max's mistake. "You're thinking of someone else."

"You mean," said Max, his puzzled frown deepening, "you're not the graduate student I've been expecting from the University of Indiana?"

"No, I'm not," said Julie, beginning to feel a nervous tightening in the pit of her stomach. She moistened her lips. It appeared that she might have to show her hand before dinner after all.

"Hmm, I just naturally assumed that you were," said Max. He gazed into the forest, as if searching his memory. "Come to think of it, the name on the resume was Karen Something-or-other, not Julie Winlock." He again regarded Julie, with an expression of piqued curiosity. "We usually don't get drop-ins at Manu River."

"No, I suppose not," said Julie, with a short ripple of nervous laughter. "It's pretty remote. It took me four days to get here."

"So if you're not Karen What's-her-name," said Max, "who are you exactly, and why have you come here?"

"I was planning to explain everything," said Julie, with an anxious swallow, "but I was putting it off until after dinner."

"Putting it off?" said Max. "Why would you do that?"

"I guess I didn't want to upset you," said Julie, with a little shrug.

"Upset me?" said Max. A guarded expression came over his face. "What are you talking about?"

"Can't it wait until we get back to the research station?" said Julie, still hoping to delve into the touchy subject at a more auspicious time.

"No," said Max, with an air of finality, "I'm afraid it can't wait."

He planted his feet on the path and crossed his arms over his broad chest. His eyes skewered Julie with a look that demanded answers.

"Tell me what's going on, Julie," he said. "You may as well upset me right here and now and get it over with."

Julie, still gathering her thoughts, said nothing for a moment.

"You and I are not taking one more step," said Max, clearly meaning business, "until you explain yourself."

"But it's getting dark," said Julie, hoping to distract him.

"I don't care," he said, in the cool voice of indifference. "We both have flashlights. I'm prepared to stay out here until midnight, if that's what it takes."

"But I'd really rather—"

"Come on, Julie," said Max, his tone taking on the sharp edge of impatience. "You're wasting time. No one, certainly not someone on her own, pops up at the research station without a good reason. You led me to believe that you were here to study, and then you—"

"I *am* here to study," she said, interrupting him. "Partly, that is. I want to learn all I can about this area."

"Then you wander off and get yourself lost," continued Max, ignoring Julie's comment as he continued to count off her irritating misdemeanors. "I've spent valuable time out looking for you, worrying that you might've fallen into the river or run into a hungry jaguar."

"I told you I was sorry," said Julie, feeling a spurt of anger.

"I am the director of the research station," said Max, waving aside her apology. "Do you know what that means? It means that I am responsible for everyone and for everything that happens here."

"I know that."

"No one can work at the station or visit here," said Max, "without prior approval." He pinned her in place with a steely, take-no-prisoners gaze. "I don't know who you are or why you're here, but you are going to tell me all about that right now."

Julie tried to steady her nerves. Things were not going according to plan, at all. She'd wanted to use finesse and diplomacy with Max when she revealed the purpose of her visit. But he was obviously not going to give her that chance. She took a deep breath and plunged in.

"All right," she said, "I work for the Pierson-Roth Foundation."

Max said nothing, but Julie watched as his face darkened and his lips formed a tight, tense line. She'd already touched a raw nerve, simply by mentioning the name of the organization that funded the Manu River Research Station.

"Didn't you get their e-mail," she asked, "telling you that I was on my way? You were supposed to be contacted several days ago."

"There's been no e-mail," said Max, shaking his head. A muscle twitched in his jaw.

"Well," said Julie, feeling at a loss, "someone at the Foundation apparently dropped the ball. My showing up like this has obviously caught you off guard. I'm sorry about that."

"Go on."

"I've come here from Seattle," she said, forging ahead, "to gather information and then write a report for Pierson-Roth."

"A report about what?" he said.

"About how to implement some changes at Manu River," said

Julie. She paused. "I believe you already know what the board of directors wants."

"I know what they want," said Max, glowering from beneath lowered brows. He gave an impatient huff of breath. "And they already know that I'm totally against their ridiculous plan."

He regarded Julie with eyes as cold and blue as glacier ice.

"So," he continued, with a slow nod of his head, "they've sent you to do their dirty work for them. I get it. You're supposed to talk sense into me." His expression hardened. "Am I right?"

"Sort of," admitted Julie, feeling acutely uncomfortable. She'd been warned that Max was resisting the Foundation's ideas for expansion, but she'd not been prepared to feel so caught in the middle of such a hot issue.

"Are you a scientist?" said Max, barking out the query like a challenge.

"No," said Julie, "I have a background in business management and public relations."

"Well, this just gets better and better," said Max, tossing up his hands in a gesture of utter disbelief. "Let's see if I have this right. Pierson-Roth sends someone down here who isn't even a scientist, and expects that person, who knows nothing about the work that goes on here, to convince me, the *scientist* who's run the station for eight years, about what this place needs." He shook his head. "That is just plain unbelievable. Not to mention insulting," he added.

"You mustn't be insulted," said Julie, trying to placate him. "The members of the board have absolute faith in you. In fact, they're adamant about your continuing to run the research station indefinitely."

Max said nothing. Instead, he just shook his head again and raked his fingers through his hair. The disheveled ebony locks matched his dark, agitated mood.

"The board trusts you," Julie went on, "and they appreciate how dedicated you are." She moistened her lips. "They believe in your good judgment. But they also recognize that you and they have a basic disagreement about the upcoming changes."

"You've got that right," snapped Max.

"Which is why they hired me," said Julie, maintaining her composure. "And while we're on the subject, the report that I'll be writing does not require a science background. I'll need your input, of course," she added, "but skills in management and public relations are what's needed at this point."

"Public relations," muttered Max, as if the term left a sour taste in his mouth. "I'll fight them, you know," he said, sounding as grimly determined as a gladiator sharpening his weapon.

Julie watched Max's eyes turn flinty with anger.

"Are you aware," he said, biting off his words, "that not one member of the Pierson-Roth Foundation has ever come down here to see this place for themselves? They fund the work we do here, but they've never been to Manu River."

Julie listened, saying nothing.

"They're basically good people," continued Max, his tone softening a shade, "and very well intentioned. I'm grateful for their support." He regarded Julie. "But what can *they* possibly tell *me* about what's best for this place?"

"That's my job," said Julie. "I'm the Foundation's eyes and ears for now. My written report, as well as my photos and drawings, will tell the board members all they need to know. They don't have to come down here."

She paused and then decided to take a chance on him.

"I hope you'll work with me on this, Max," she said.

"I'll be civil, if that's what you mean," he said, exhaling with annoyance. "But we're on opposite sides of a very touchy situation, Julie. You're not going to change my mind. And, if I have to fight the board through you, well, so be it."

"I'm sorry to have told you this way," said Julie, trying to make peace. "I knew you'd be upset. That's why I wanted to save it for after dinner. We're both hungry and tired. This could've waited until later."

"Even if I'd eaten a four-course meal," said Max, scowling, "and gotten ten hours of sleep, I'd still not be happy to learn why you're here." He gave an impatient shrug. "Tell me now, tell me later. It's all the same."

The fight suddenly drained out of Julie. "Okay, Max," she said, holding up her hands in a gesture of surrender, "I get it. But let's call a truce for now, shall we?" She glanced around at the shadowy forest. "It's getting late, and I need to eat some real food soon or I'll faint."

She hazarded a little smile, hoping to lighten the combative mood that had tainted the atmosphere.

"Aren't you hungry, Max?" she said.

"I *was* hungry," he said, with a curt nod of his head.

Then, without another word, he turned and began stalking up the trail.

Sighing to herself, Julie fell in behind him for a silent trudge back to the research station.

Chapter Three

W here's your luggage, Julie?" said Max, as the two of them entered a clearing near the river.

The clearing held several modest wooden buildings with thatched roofs and screened porches. Boardwalks and tidy dirt paths connected the buildings. Palms, flowering shrubs, and tropical grasses served as natural landscaping. A hand-painted sign on the main building read MANU RIVER RESEARCH STATION.

"My luggage?" said Julie, pausing to catch her breath. "I left it in the dining hall."

Max had set a brisk pace on their hike back to the research station. Several times, Julie had had to trot a few steps to keep up with his long strides. She hadn't dared to ask him to slow down, however, for fear of igniting another spirited debate.

Max hadn't spoken a word since their heated exchange on the trail. He'd stalked along the path in silence, his body language radiating displeasure.

But now, in the clearing, Julie could hear in Max's voice that his anger over her surprise visit had abated. He'd apparently walked off some of his ire during their march through

30

the forest. She was glad of that, yet she knew that their conflict was far from over.

"I only brought a duffel bag," said Julie. "I'll get it later."

"As you like," said Max. "I suppose I should give you a quick tour of camp before it gets dark," he added. "We've got a few minutes left."

"Thanks, I'd like that."

"So, tell me something," said Max, shifting his weight from one hip to the other. "For how long will we have the, uh, pleasure of your company?"

Julie noted that his tone was not unfriendly. But it wasn't exactly warmly welcoming either. She knew that her presence there was a thorn in Max's side, and that he was probably seething about it just below the surface. But she could see that he'd decided to extend, however reluctantly, some common courtesies. She was secretly thankful that he'd risen to the occasion, even if he was only pretending to be a good host.

"How long will I be here?" said Julie. She gave a little shrug. "I'm not sure. I guess it depends."

"On what?" said Max, his blue eyes fixed on her.

"On how long it takes me to gather all the information I need," said Julie. "I want my report to be as complete as possible."

"Humph," grunted Max, his jaw tightening.

There was an uncomfortable silence.

"Look, I'm sorry to show up like this," said Julie. "I know you weren't expecting me."

"Don't apologize," said Max, gruffly brushing her comment aside. "It's not your fault that no one bothered to tell me you were coming. There's been some kind of breakdown in communications. I don't blame you for that."

"I appreciate it," said Julie, with a little smile. "Still, I don't want to cause you any trouble or inconvenience."

"You're too late to avoid that," said Max, one dark brow

arching with irony. "You've already caused me trouble and inconvenience."

Then he, too, flashed a half smile.

"But, look," he continued, the accusing edge leaving his voice, "you're here now, so we'll just have to make the most of it."

Julie nodded.

"Let me show you around," said Max. He gestured toward the structure with the sign over the door. "That's our main building. As you already know, it contains the dining hall and kitchen. There's also a small library, various work spaces, and a room for meetings and lectures."

He turned and began walking along one of the boardwalks. Julie followed him, admiring the strong outline of his shoulders, the lean silhouette of his hips, and the leonine grace of his stride. She moistened her lips, trying to keep her mind on business.

They stopped beside a rustic hut with a luxuriant flowering vine growing up one wall. A sweet, heady fragrance, like that of gardenias with a hint of vanilla, filled the air.

Just then, some movement caught Julie's attention.

"Look," she cried, with delight, "a hummingbird."

A flying jewel no bigger than Julie's thumb zipped over to the vine and plunged its slender beak into one of the blossoms. Its tiny wings were a blur as it hovered in place.

"What kind of hummingbird is it?" said Julie, as she watched the bird dart from flower to flower in its quest for nectar.

"*Chlorostilbon mellisugus,*" said Max, his eyes on the creature, as well.

Julie laughed. "In English, please."

"Oh, that's right," said Max, snapping his fingers as if he'd suddenly remembered something. "I completely forgot that you're not a *scientist.*"

"Ouch," said Julie, but she'd caught the twinkle in Max's eye. "You can't resist reminding me, can you?" she added, teasing him in return.

"I'm just making a point," he said, throwing up his hands in mock defense.

"Well, now I'll make a point," said Julie, lightly tapping Max's chest with her forefinger. "You don't have to be a scientist to appreciate a hummingbird."

"That is true," said Max, giving a little nod.

"So, Mister Ornithology," said Julie, tilting her head to look up into his eyes, "what do people like me call this little beauty?"

"Its common name," said Max, "is blue-tailed emerald."

"Oh, that's perfect," said Julie, returning her gaze to the lustrous green hummingbird with the blue tail feathers. "It really does look like an emerald on wings."

"Here, I'll show you something," said Max. "Turn around."

Julie faced Max and then felt his hands on her bare arms. The touch of his palms molding to the curve of her shoulders ignited a deep hunger in Julie. She pressed her lips together and shivered with pleasure.

"Now step back against the vine," said Max, using his hands to guide her.

When Julie was in place, Max plucked one of the flowers. He carefully swept Julie's hair away from her face, his warm fingers grazing her cheeks, and then he tucked the flower behind her ear.

The cool satin of the flower petals brushed Julie's heated skin. An intoxicating fragrance, rising from the deep, velvety throat of the flower, aroused her senses.

With a jolt of tender yearning, Julie was suddenly reminded of the countless little gestures that flow between lovers. The sharing of a flower was such a simple act, and yet it often carried a much deeper meaning. She marveled at her thoughts. After all, she barely knew Max. Still, she couldn't deny that she was powerfully drawn to him.

Max stepped back.

"Now don't move a muscle," he said in a quiet voice. "Just stand right there and wait."

Within seconds, the hummingbird darted back to the vine, lured by the promise of sweet nectar.

Julie held her breath and tried to keep from blinking, lest she startle the little creature.

The hummingbird flew closer and closer.

Then, out of the corner of her eye, Julie watched as the bird thrust its beak into the blossom nestled in her hair. The air stirred against her cheek, fanned by the bird's whirring wings.

Satisfied, the hummingbird backed away from the flower. Then it hovered a few inches in front of Julie's face. For an astonishing moment or two, Julie was eye to eye with one of nature's most enchanting creatures.

Giving Julie a final curious look, the blue-tailed emerald zipped away and vanished into the dusk.

"That was pure magic," said Julie, expelling her breath in a sigh of awe. She was touched by the fact that Max had staged a unique experience that he knew would charm her. "I'm going to remember that for the rest of my life," she said. "Thank you, Max."

He just smiled. Then he shifted back into tour-guide mode.

"This is our lounge," he said, indicating the hut on which the vine was growing. A sign on the door read THE WATERING HOLE. Max chuckled. "It's nothing fancy, but it has the distinction of being the only bar for three hundred miles in any direction."

"I'm impressed," said Julie, nodding.

"But don't expect cold drinks," he went on. "The only refrigerator we've got is in the kitchen, and it's reserved for food only. It runs off a generator," he added.

"Hmm," said Julie, nodding.

"So I hope you like your beer warm," said Max, slanting a smile in Julie's direction.

She laughed.

Then she leaned toward the door to read something. Beneath the sign, etched into the wooden planks with a black marker,

were scrawled the words, WHAT HAPPENS IN THE JUNGLE STAYS
IN THE JUNGLE.

"That," said Max, referring to the message, "was put there
last year by a graduate student with a wicked sense of humor."
He laughed. "Pay no attention."

He started to walk on and then paused.

"Oh, before we continue our tour," he said, "I should probably mention Lucy." There was a playful gleam in his eye.

"Lucy?" said Julie. "Who's that, one of the students?"

"No, Lucy's not a student," said Max, with an air of mystery. He stroked his chin. "She's more of a teacher, actually."

"Will I get to meet her?" said Julie.

"Oh, you'll meet Lucy," said Max. He gestured toward the
hut. "She lives in the lounge and she's very friendly."

"Sorry, you've lost me," said Julie. She tilted her head at
Max. "Are you just making this up?"

"Nope," said Max, "Lucy's as real as you and me. And," he
added, "I've never met anyone who didn't like her. You'll see."

"Hmm," said Julie, feeling both puzzled and intrigued.

"No more hints," said Max, flashing her a smile. "Now, on
with the tour."

They proceeded along the boardwalk.

"How many graduate students are here now?" asked Julie.

"Only four," said Max, talking over his shoulder as they
walked single file. "Those are their quarters over there," he
added, pointing out a row of neat little cabins. "We've got a
very dedicated bunch. Noelle is studying the dynamics of ant
swarms, and Ted's conducting a survey of rain forest moths."
He paused. "Then we have our current resident sweethearts,
Fran and Robert."

"Sweethearts?" said Julie.

"Fran and Robert are from two different universities," said
Max. "They met at Manu River and fell in love."

"Does that happen often?" said Julie, her ears perking up.
"People falling in love here, I mean."

"You'd be surprised," said Max, with an indulgent chuckle. "But it's understandable."

"What do you mean?" said Julie, her curiosity piqued.

"Well, think about it," said Max, as the boardwalk made a turn. "We're out here in the middle of nowhere, miles away from television and shopping malls and all the other trappings of civilization."

"There are no distractions," said Julie, nodding.

"That's right," said Max. "It's a simple, pared-down lifestyle at Manu River. The graduate students who come here to study are in each other's company around the clock. They work, eat, and play together. They're having the adventure of a lifetime, and they all have one big thing in common."

"A passion for the rain forest," said Julie.

"Exactly," said Max. "Put a group like that in a setting like this, and, well, sparks of attraction are bound to fly eventually. And, before you know it, some of them have fallen in love."

"I see what you mean," said Julie.

"Given the circumstances," said Max, "I'm actually surprised when that *doesn't* happen."

"It's the rule of 'like plus energy,'" murmured Julie.

"Excuse me?" said Max, glancing back at her.

"Oh, I was just remembering an article I once read," said Julie. "It was about falling in love. The point was made that if you like someone and then put time and energy into the relationship, there's a very good chance that you and that other person will fall in love. Even if you hadn't meant to," she added.

"Hmm," said Max, nodding, "that makes sense."

Julie thought she detected a wistful note in Max's voice. The subject of falling in love may have stirred up unhappy memories for him. Back in the forest, he'd briefly mentioned a former wife. Was he still in love with her?

"So, what are Fran and Robert studying here?" said Julie. "Besides each other, that is," she added, with a mischievous laugh.

"They're filming a documentary," said Max. "It's on giant river otters."

"That sounds interesting," said Julie. She thought for a moment. "Giant river otters are rare, aren't they?"

"They're *very* rare," said Max, "which is why studying them is essential. Luckily, we know of two or three family groups in some oxbow sections of the Manu River, not too far from here."

"Hmm."

"Fran and Robert's documentary," continued Max, "will shed light on the otters' chances for survival. I don't mean just for the otters living in the national park," he added, "where they have some protection. I'm talking about the species as a whole."

"I see," said Julie. "That's important work."

Max stopped and then turned to face her.

"Yes, it is," he said, leveling a steady gaze at her, "and I hope you'll include that information in your report."

"Of course."

"And I also hope," said Max, with a sober expression, "that you'll consider how vital it is that such research goes forward without interference." He shifted his weight. "Put *that* in your paper."

"I plan to write a balanced, unbiased report," said Julie, trying not to sound defensive. "The facts will speak for themselves." She paused. "The Pierson-Roth Foundation is obviously already aware of the wonderful work being done here, Max. Why else would they have funded the research station all these years?"

"They've been a huge support," said Max, conceding the point. "In fact, they've been our *only* support. I appreciate all they've done. Of course I do."

Julie was listening.

"But now they're trying to force a ridiculous plan down my throat," he went on, sounding frustrated. "If they get their way, this place will be changed forever. The priorities just wouldn't be the same. What we're trying to accomplish here would go right down the drain."

Julie could see that Max was working up a head of steam over the matter. She braced herself for another round of heated debate.

"The board members," she said, "are only trying to do what's best for Manu River."

Max's eyes blazed.

"Opening the research station to tourists," he said, from between compressed lips, "is *not* what's best for Manu River."

"But in today's economy," said Julie, trying to appeal to Max's practical side, "money is tight and getting tighter. Inviting ecotourists to visit the station would bring in revenue." She paused. "You may not like the idea, Max, but even you must see that tourist dollars would help keep this place afloat."

"We do serious, important work here," said Max, emphasizing each word. "Manu River is for *scientists,* not for a bunch of loud-talking tourists wearing straw hats and flowered shirts."

"I can hardly believe my ears," remarked Julie, laughing. "Straw hats and flowered shirts?" She clucked her tongue in mock disapproval. "Shame on you, Max. What a silly stereotype."

"Yes, I know that," said Max, with a dismissive gesture, "and I used it on purpose. I'm just trying to make a point, that's all."

"Which is?"

"Which is," he said, "that tourists would only get in the way. Besides," he went on, "there're already plenty of eco-lodges in Peru and Ecuador and Brazil." He gave an impatient wave of his hand. "If people want to come to South America to have a 'jungle experience,' they can go to one of those places."

"But this area is unique," said Julie. "It isn't like anyplace else, from what I can tell."

"That's right," said Max. "Manu River is unique and unspoiled, and I intend to keep it that way."

There was an uncomfortable silence.

"I don't get it," said Julie. "What do you have against eco-tourists?"

"Not a thing," said Max, shrugging. "I've been an ecotourist myself a couple of times. I just happen to believe that tourism and pure science don't mix, that's all. This is a very special place, Julie. It would kill me to see people trampling through here."

"What makes you so sure that—"

"You know what?" said Max, interrupting Julie with an abruptly raised hand. "I don't mean to be rude, but I've had enough of this topic for one day. We don't agree, so let's leave it at that."

Julie bit back a comment that had leaped to her tongue and said nothing.

"I have a lot of work waiting for me in my office," said Max, "and I should get to it." He began walking. "Come on," he tossed over his shoulder, sounding as if he could hardly wait to have her off his hands, "I'll show you to your cabin."

Julie stared at Max's retreating back for a moment. Was he always this stubborn? Convincing him to see the wisdom in the Foundation's plan was going to be harder than she'd thought.

She heaved a sigh of frustration and then ran to catch up with him.

It was dark by the time Max and Julie reached a cabin standing by itself in a quiet corner of the clearing. The wooden structure rested on vertical posts, several feet above the ground. Steps led up to a screened-in front porch.

Max shed the beam of his flashlight on the steps. Then he and Julie mounted the steps and entered the cabin.

Max flipped a wall switch, illuminating an overhead light fixture. He doused his flashlight and turned to regard Julie.

"This is where you'll be staying," he said. His tone was brisk and businesslike. "We have electricity from six to ten each night," he explained. "It runs off a generator. If you need any light after ten, you'll have to use one of those."

He nodded toward a shelf, on which sat an old-fashioned lantern with a wick and a glass chimney. Nearby sat a tray holding candles and matches.

"The lantern's a bit primitive," said Max, "but it works." He glanced at Julie. "You *do* know how to use a kerosene lantern, don't you?"

"Yes."

"Good," said Max, giving a brief nod. "Just don't burn the place down, all right?"

Julie rolled her eyes at him, half in jest.

"I'm not trying to talk down to you," said Max, catching her expression. "Everyone who stays at Manu River gets the same lecture. It's almost impossible to fight fires here. I don't want to spend money replacing a cabin."

"Relax," said Julie, briefly touching his arm, "you're talking to a former Girl Scout." She smiled. "I'll be careful."

"Okay, then," he said, "I won't worry."

"This is really nice," said Julie, looking around at the combination bedroom and sitting area.

The space was clean and functional, with the lemony scent of polished wood. Screened windows on all sides kept out the mosquitoes, while allowing the mysterious sounds and smells of the jungle to drift into the room.

The furnishings consisted of a table and two chairs, a settee with a woven rush bottom, a double bed, and a bedside table. Shelves lined one wall, where Julie could store her clothing and personal items.

Just then, a spot of movement caught her eye.

"Oh, look," she said. "What's that little thing?"

She pointed toward a small, green, lizard-shaped creature that was clinging high up one wall, near the ceiling.

"That's a member of the *Gekkonidae* family," said Max.

"Hey, I'm not a scientist, remember?" said Julie, in mock rebuke.

"Yeah, I keep forgetting," growled Max, raising one brow. "It's a gecko," he said. "You'll see a lot of those. This one and its friend over there"—he gestured toward another gecko, poised on a window ledge—"will catch any flies or other creepy-crawlies you might have in here."

"That's useful," said Julie. She smiled. "I've never seen a gecko before. They're awfully cute."

"Geckos sometimes chirp at night," said Max. "I hope the chirping doesn't keep you awake."

Julie gave a weary laugh. "I doubt that anything could keep me awake tonight," she said. "I'm bushed."

"The bathroom's through there," said Max, indicating a door across the room. "It's got everything you need—sink, flush-toilet, shower. The hot water for the shower comes from a solar-tank behind the cabin."

"I'm amazed," said Julie.

"What do you mean?" said Max.

"Hot water and a flush-toilet?" she said. "I wasn't expecting such comfortable digs out here in the rain forest. Even the bed's a nice surprise."

"What were you expecting?" said Max, a quizzical look on his face.

"I guess I pictured hammocks and outdoor latrines," said Julie.

"And yet you were still willing to come here?" said Max, studying her face. "Even though you thought it might be as primitive as all that?"

"Sure," said Julie, with a little shrug. "It sounded like an adventure. I assumed I'd have to rough it, and I knew I couldn't be picky about the conditions. After all, I have a job to do."

"There's *that* topic again," grunted Max, frowning.

Julie quickly changed the subject.

"I know I'll be comfortable here, Max," she said, keeping her tone light. "This is all so new and exciting. I can't wait to see what it's like to sleep in the middle of a tropical rain forest."

Max studied her for a moment and then muttered something under his breath.

"Excuse me?" said Julie.

"Oh, I was just remembering something," said Max, rubbing a hand across the back of his neck. "My wife hated this place. She visited Manu River only once and she was miserable the whole time she was here."

"Why?" asked Julie, listening with interest.

"She was completely out of her element," said Max. "The climate didn't suit her, she was unhappy with the basic accommodations, and she was bored out of her mind."

"I see."

"And there was no way," said Max, with a rueful sigh, "that she would've shared a room with a gecko. They made her nervous, she said, and she couldn't sleep."

"Well," said Julie, choosing her words carefully, "I hope she found something to enjoy."

"Nope," said Max, shaking his head. "Barbara couldn't stand it here. She finally cut her visit short and went home early. I can't say that I blame her."

Julie nodded, saying nothing.

"Of course, her reaction disappointed me," continued Max. "I was hoping she'd like Manu River as much as I do." He paused. "Oh, well, it was my fault for dragging her out here. I should've known that the rain forest wouldn't be her cup of tea."

"Hmm."

"Hey," said Max, as if jolting his thoughts back to the present, "why am I rehashing ancient history? You don't need to hear this. I'm divorced now, and I should leave the past where it belongs." He let out his breath. "Sorry to bend your ear, Julie."

"Don't apologize," said Julie. "Everyone needs to get things off their chest now and then." She regarded Max, curious to know more about him. "Do you have children, Max?"

"No," he said, shaking his head. "How about you?"

"No," said Julie.

There was a reflective pause.

"Speaking of spouses," said Max, breaking the silence, "why didn't you bring your husband along?"

"My husband?" said Julie, startled by the reference.

"Sure, why not?" said Max. He gestured toward the double bed. "There's room here for two people." He raised one brow and gave Julie a pointed look. "One more—how shall I put it?—unexpected guest wouldn't have made any difference."

"I don't have a husband," said Julie, as she felt a by-then-familiar lump rising in her throat.

"No husband?" said Max, looking confused. "But you're wearing a ring," he continued, nodding toward the gold wedding band on Julie's left hand. "I assumed you were married."

"I *was* married," said Julie, "but now I'm a widow." She swallowed. It was still so hard to say those words. "My husband died just over a year ago. It was very sudden, and I—"

She looked down at her ring and stumbled over her words.

"I just haven't had the heart to take this off," she continued. "I will eventually, I suppose, when the time feels right."

There was an awkward silence, broken only by the melodic humming of nighttime insects drifting through the window screens.

"Wow, me and my big mouth," said Max, in a self-accusing tone.

He walked over to Julie, closing the gap between them, and laid a reassuring hand on her arm.

"I didn't mean to bring up sad memories for you," he said. "I'm sorry, Julie."

"It's okay," she said, blinking away some unshed tears. "You didn't know."

Julie marveled at how the touch of Max's warm hand on her

arm took the edge off her mournful thoughts. The reaching out of a friendly hand was a simple act, she mused, and yet it conveyed such a powerful message of empathy and support.

At that moment, standing close to Max, Julie felt a deep personal connection with him. They'd both been through tough times and had coped with disappointment. They were seasoned travelers on the road of life, learning hard lessons and emerging wiser from them. As she looked into his compassionate eyes, she instinctively knew that Max, regardless of what had happened in his past, was a man a woman could count on.

Just then, one of the geckos gave a little chirp. The cheerful sound broke the spell of the moment and caused Julie to chuckle with delight.

"I should get going," said Max, glancing at his watch. He stepped toward the door. "Dinner's in half an hour. Oh, and if you need anything, see Hernando's wife Isabel. She's in charge of housekeeping and laundry."

Julie nodded.

"Just don't get *too* comfortable," said Max, reverting to his businesslike tone.

"What's that supposed to mean?" said Julie.

"Do you remember the graduate student I mentioned?" said Max. "The one coming here from the University of Indiana?"

"Karen," said Julie, nodding.

"That's the one," said Max. "She's arriving a week from now and this is where she'll be staying, in this cabin. She specifically requested a double bed, because her husband plans to join her later to help with her field studies."

"I see," said Julie.

"So what I'm asking," said Max, "is that you please take care of your, uh, business at Manu River as quickly as possible, so that you can vacate this cabin when Karen gets here. In fact," he added, "it would be handy if you could take the same boat out that'll be delivering her. It'll save the boat guys from having to make an extra trip."

"But that only gives me a few days," said Julie.

"That should be more than enough time," said Max. He regarded her. "As far as that goes, you could practically write your report for the Foundation tonight."

"What do you mean?" said Julie.

"You already know the basics," said Max, with a cool shrug. "Manu River is a place for serious work and research, and its director—that would be *me*—is totally opposed to any activities that would compromise its mission. That's the heart of the matter, Julie. It won't take you more than a day or two to fill in some details, and then you can be out of here."

"I'm sure I'll need more than a week," said Julie, beginning to feel as if Max was unfairly pressuring her. "I told you that I want my report to be complete and unbiased. That'll take time. I need to collect data, make an informal survey of the area, find out what's going on here, and so on."

"I've already told you what's going on here," said Max, his voice taking on an argumentative edge.

"Yes," said Julie, holding her ground, "and you've also made your opinion very clear. But I need to see things for myself. I need to take pictures and work up some diagrams and sketches. I want to poke around and explore and talk to the students." She gestured with her hands. "I want to learn everything I can about Manu River."

"If you stay here longer than a week," said Max, his jaw muscles twitching with annoyance, "where, exactly, would you plan to sleep?"

"Oh, I'll figure something out," said Julie, with a nonchalant shrug. "Maybe I can bunk with one of the women grad students."

"Everyone's already doubled up," said Max, "and we're using the spare cabins for storage at the moment."

"Okay," said Julie, "then I'll sleep in the dining hall, if I have to."

"What, on the floor?" said Max, frowning.

"Sure, why not?" said Julie.

"But you'd be uncomfortable," said Max.

"Yes, you're probably right," said Julie, with a short laugh, "but I can handle it. This is all new to me, but I can adapt, if necessary."

"You wouldn't last two nights," said Max.

"Is that a challenge?" said Julie, lifting her chin while keeping her tone pleasant. "Because if it is," she added, "game on."

Max glowered at her, seeming at a loss for words.

"Look," said Julie, trying to pacify him, "I'm only trying to do my job, Max. Work with me."

Max's expression remained stony.

"I'm here for however long it takes," said Julie, leveling a businesslike gaze at him. "I don't mean to sound pushy or unfriendly, but you'd better get used to the idea. And," she added, in a lighter tone, "I'd really appreciate your cooperation."

"I suppose I *have* to cooperate," said Max, from between tight lips, "but I'll only go as far as I have to. Beyond that, you're on your own."

"Fair enough," said Julie, happy for the concession, however reluctantly offered.

"And," said Max, stabbing the air for emphasis, "don't expect me to like it."

With that he turned on his heel and left the cabin, allowing the screen door to close with a bang.

Julie listened to the sound of Max's footfalls on the steps outside. Then she ran out to the porch and called after him.

"Will I see you at dinner, Max?"

But he was already gone.

Chapter Four

Julie washed her hands and face after Max stalked away from her cabin. Later, when she went outside, intent on retrieving her duffel bag, she found that the boardwalk had been illuminated with softly glowing lanterns spaced every few feet.

The lantern-trail cast a magical spell on the ebony night. Stars twinkling in the sky lent their celestial charm to the scene as well. As Julie walked along the boardwalk, she breathed deeply of the pungent night air, listened to the sound of singing crickets, and felt at one with her surroundings.

Near the dining hall, she exchanged greetings with an older Peruvian man whose nightly job it was to light the lanterns. The worker, named Pablo, spoke little English. Chatting with Pablo gave Julie a chance to brush up on her high school Spanish.

When Julie continued on her way, she felt a surge of optimism. If she could figure out how to communicate with Max as easily as she'd spoken with Pablo in his native language, her battle to influence Max's thinking about the future for Manu River would be half won.

The dining hall was deserted, but Julie could smell the

tantalizing aroma of food cooking. She poked her head into the kitchen, where she found Hernando preparing a platter of tropical fruit. Hernando's helper, a young man who introduced himself as Cesar, was tending some pots on the stove.

Julie expressed her appreciation to Hernando for having observed which path she'd taken upon her arrival. Thanks to him, Max had known where to look for Julie, saving her from an uncomfortable night in the rain forest.

Hernando graciously accepted Julie's thanks and then offered her a slice of fresh mango. The mango was sweet and juicy. Its exotic flavor lingered in Julie's mouth as she carried her duffel bag back to her cabin.

Julie quickly unpacked and arranged her belongings on the shelves. Then she changed into some different pants and put on a long-sleeved shirt over her tank top.

In the bathroom, Julie brushed her hair in front of the mirror. She considered tying her hair back with a scarf, and then decided to leave it loose and flowing around her face and shoulders.

In the back of her mind, Julie remembered that Max admired her long hair. She wasn't intending to flirt with Max or to go out of her way to draw his attention. But she saw no harm in making a small concession with her appearance by leaving her hair the way it was.

After applying some lipstick and giving her image in the mirror a final inspection, she was ready to go.

When Julie entered the dining hall this time, she found it ringing with the sounds of laughter and lively conversation. Four young university students were sitting at a candlelit table set for dinner. Noticing Julie, the students called out for her to join them. She took a place at the table and introduced herself.

"Hi, my name's Julie," she said, looking around at the friendly, curious faces.

"Pleased to meet you," said one of the students, a young woman with dark hair cut into a pixie style. "I'm Noelle," she said, smiling. "Welcome to Manu River."

"Thank you," Julie said, and regarded the young woman. "You're studying ants, as I recall."

"Ah, your reputation precedes you, Noelle," said one of the male students, in a playful, theatrical manner. He gave Julie an owlish look. "In case you ever forget Noelle's obsession with the *Formicidae* family, a glance at her wrist will remind you."

Noelle laughed and held out her left arm for Julie to see. Encircling her wrist was a tattooed "bracelet" of ants, marching end to end like links in a chain.

"This tattoo was a birthday gift from my boyfriend," explained Noelle. "These are leafcutter ants, my favorites."

"I'm Ted, by the way," said the male student. He had brown hair, and he was wearing a faded T-shirt bearing the message A LEPIDOPTERIST CAN MAKE YOUR HEART FLUTTER. He gave a dramatic flourish with his hand. "I'm the resident moth man."

"I see," said Julie, returning his smile.

"And these two," continued Ted, indicating a couple sitting side by side, "are a study in ornithological romance."

"I'm sorry?" said Julie, enjoying the friendly banter.

"He means they're lovebirds," said Noelle, with a good-natured roll of her eyes at Ted's play on words.

"Exactly," said Ted. "Her name is Fran and his is Robert. When they're not whispering silly romantic things in each other's ears, they're filming giant river otters."

"That must be challenging," said Julie, addressing the pair. "How's it going?"

"It's going very well," said Fran, with enthusiasm. A mop of light brown hair framed her face in curly confusion. "We got some great footage today of a female otter teaching its young how to catch fish."

Fran's boyfriend Robert nodded in agreement. His long blond hair was pulled back into a ponytail, and he wore a small gold hoop in one ear.

"So, what are you studying, Julie?" asked Noelle, as Hernando and Cesar began delivering food to the table.

"Oh, I'm not a student," said Julie, as they passed around the serving bowls. She ladled rice and chicken stew onto her plate. "I work for the Pierson-Roth Foundation."

"Oh, yeah, Pierson-Roth," said Ted, reaching for a warm dinner roll. "That's the organization that funds the research station, isn't it?"

"That's right," said Julie, helping herself to some steamed vegetables. "I'm here to gather data and write a report for the Foundation."

"What kind of report?" asked Ted, buttering his roll.

"It'll be sort of an overview," said Julie.

She was purposely keeping her remarks general, for she sensed that Max had not shared the Foundation's ecotourism plan with the students. They were in the dark about the changes coming to Manu River, and Julie thought it best to keep things that way. At least for now. If Max wanted the students filled in, it was his place to tell them and not Julie's.

"I'll need a lot of input," said Julie, glancing around the table. "I hope you'll all give me a hand with that."

"Sure," said Fran, and everyone else nodded in agreement.

The five of them ate in silence for a few minutes. Then Noelle spoke up.

"Where's our fearless leader?" she said, nodding toward an empty chair and an untouched place setting. "If Max doesn't get here soon, he's going to miss dinner."

Julie had also been wondering about Max. While she was eating, she'd glanced several times toward the door, expecting to see him. But, so far, he hadn't shown up. Where was he?

Julie had been looking forward to sharing a relaxed meal with Max. She'd planned to keep their conversation light and general, knowing that good food and congenial company could sometimes help to bridge the gap between adversaries.

But as the meal progressed and Max still didn't appear, Julie realized, with disappointment, that she wasn't going to have a chance for some friendly give-and-take with him over dinner after all. Not that night, anyway.

"I saw Max heading toward the lounge," said Ted. "He seemed a little grumpy."

"Doctor Max grumpy?" said Fran, looking surprised.

"He's never grumpy," said Robert, between bites of food.

"Well, he is tonight," said Ted, spearing a chunk of pineapple from the fruit platter.

"Hmm, that's weird," muttered Noelle.

There was another silence at the table, broken only by the sounds of cutlery clinking against china. Julie kept her eyes on her plate, hoping the others wouldn't notice the flush that she felt warming her cheeks. She could guess why Max was "grumpy," and why he'd apparently decided to forgo dinner. His latest verbal skirmish with Julie, at her cabin, had put him into a foul mood and now he was probably avoiding her.

"It isn't like Max to skip a meal," said Fran. "He was out on the river all day. He's got to be hungry."

"One of us should take him some food," said Noelle.

"I was just thinking the same thing myself," said Julie. "I'll do it." She reached for the empty dinner plate and began spooning chicken and rice onto it.

"Maybe you can cheer him up at the same time," said Ted, around a mouthful of mango.

"Well, I'm not sure about that," said Julie, with a little shrug, "but I'll do my best."

A few minutes later, Julie left the dining hall carrying a covered plate of food and some cutlery. She walked along the boardwalk to the Watering Hole, feeling nervous. She was taking a chance and she knew it. What kind of reception would she get from Max?

All things considered, Julie was probably the last person Max wanted to see. How would he react to her intrusion on his solitude? Would he be gracious, or would he express displeasure?

Bracing herself for the worst, Julie paused at the closed door of the Watering Hole. She took a deep, calming breath, filling her senses with the sweet perfume of the flowering vine growing beside the door.

She thought back. Just a couple of hours ago, Max had treated her to the most thrilling encounter she'd ever had with a hummingbird. She knew that she'd remember the experience for the rest of her life.

Julie was no longer wearing the flower that Max had placed behind her ear—she'd removed it while getting ready for dinner—but she vividly remembered how gently he'd tucked the blossom into her hair. The graze of his fingers on the sensitive skin of her cheek had stirred a deep hunger in Julie, surprising her with its intensity.

Julie knew that it wasn't fair to compare Max with her husband Simon, but she couldn't help herself. There was something about Max, an elusive quality she couldn't put her finger on, that had awakened desires in her that she'd never felt with her husband.

With Simon, Julie had enjoyed mutual love and respect and a wonderful friendship. In many ways, they'd been as close as sister and brother. Julie still missed Simon's crazy sense of humor, his boyish smile, and his easy companionship. She'd liked being married to him. But, for whatever reason, their lovemaking, although sweet and giving, had lacked passion and had always left Julie with a vague yearning for something more.

Julie stared at the door of the lounge, her mind churning. She moistened her lips. With an instinct that made her hands tremble, she knew that Max would never leave a woman wondering what she was missing.

For a moment, Julie felt guilty for having such thoughts, as if she were being disloyal to Simon's memory. At the same time, she knew for certain what her late husband would want her to do. If he could, Simon would tell Julie not to continue mourning his death, but to move on and find happiness with someone else. Simon would not only give his approval for Julie to seek a new partner, he'd give her his blessing.

Still hesitating at the door, Julie tried to sort out her feelings. Since Simon's death, Max was the first man for whom she'd felt an immediate attraction. She couldn't help but wonder if Max was drawn to her as well. There'd been a moment or two that day when she'd thought so, and yet . . .

Then Julie shook her head and gave a soft laugh of chagrin. What on earth was she thinking? She and Max were on opposite sides of a hot issue, a prickly situation that had already driven a wedge between them. Her presence there was unwelcome, to say the least. Why, Max had practically ordered her to leave in a week's time. Surely that didn't signal an interest in Julie. On the contrary, Max was probably looking forward to seeing the last of her.

Still, if there was one thing Julie had learned in the last year it was that life is full of surprises.

Acting on impulse, she picked a flower, tucked it behind her ear, and reached for the doorknob.

Julie entered the Watering Hole and softly closed the door behind her. She looked around the cozy room. It held a small bar, some tables and chairs, and a couple of wooden benches. A large painting of a jaguar and some framed photographs of rain forest birds served as wall décor.

Julie had expected to find Max in the lounge. But she must have missed him, for the room was empty. She sighed and looked down at the plate of food she'd prepared for him. *So much for good intentions,* she thought.

She was about to turn and leave when she noticed something. A door at the far end of the room stood ajar, with light streaming through the opening.

Julie called out. "Max?"

"Yes," came his deep voice, from beyond the door. "I'm on the porch." There was a pause. "Who's there?"

"It's Julie."

There was a short silence.

"Come on out," called Max, his tone neutral.

Julie crossed the room, pulled open the door, and stepped out onto a wide porch with screens on three sides. Several geckos clung to the screens, hunting insects that had been attracted to the light.

Max was comfortably slouched at a lantern-lit table with his long legs stretched in front of him, crossed at the ankles. He was wearing the same clothes as before, but had changed from waders to a pair of loafers. He'd rolled up his sleeves, exposing strong forearms lightly dusted with dark hair.

A laptop computer sat on the table in front of Max, along with a pile of papers, a can of beer, and a bowl of cashew nuts.

"Hi," said Max, drawing in his legs and sitting up as Julie walked over.

"Hi," said Julie. She gave a tentative smile. "I hope I'm not interrupting."

"It's okay," said Max, his expression impassive. "I'm ready to take a break." He gestured toward a chair. "Have a seat."

Julie gave an inward sigh of relief. Max didn't seem annoyed by her intrusion on his solitude, as she'd feared he might be. She couldn't tell for sure, but if he was sorry to see her, he was hiding the fact well.

"I met the four graduate students at dinner," said Julie, keeping her tone conversational. She seated herself at Max's table.

"What'd you think?" said Max.

"Oh, they're a great bunch of kids," said Julie, "and they're obviously very dedicated to their work."

Max nodded.

"Anyway," said Julie, "we missed you at dinner." She smiled. "Everyone thought you might starve before breakfast, so I brought you some food." She placed the covered plate and the cutlery within Max's reach.

"You didn't have to do that," said Max.

His tone was gruff around the edges, but Julie could tell that he was touched by her gesture.

"I'm not used to being waited on," he added. He slanted a teasing smile in Julie's direction. "This feels like room service. Be careful, you might spoil me."

Julie's stomach did a somersault and she felt an inner glow. She could think of a lot of ways to spoil Max.

"Well, anyway," she said, trying to cover a sudden surge of self-consciousness, "I know you'll like this. It's chicken stew."

"Ah, one of Hernando's best dishes," said Max. He pushed his laptop to one side and reached for the plate. "Nuts and beer aren't much of a meal. I was getting hungry for some real food." He looked at her. "Thanks, Julie. This was, um, really thoughtful of you."

"You're welcome," she said.

Max offered Julie some cashews and a glass of wine.

"Thanks, some other time," said Julie, shaking her head. She nodded toward the plate. "Eat your dinner, Max, while it's still warm."

Julie watched Max eat for a moment. She admired how the light from the lantern cast a golden glow on the planes of his cheeks and on the handsome curve of his brow. His head bent forward as he concentrated on the food, the picture of a man with a healthy appetite.

Julie was suddenly really glad that she'd brought food to him. She found herself wishing that she'd cooked it for him herself.

"When you didn't show up for dinner," she said, "I thought you might be avoiding me."

Max stopped chewing and glanced over at her. "Avoiding you?" he said.

"I'm sorry," said Julie, with an apologetic wave of her hand. "I shouldn't have blurted that out. Forget I said it."

"No, it's okay," said Max, swallowing his last mouthful of stew.

He pushed his empty plate to one side, wiped his lips with a napkin, and leaned back in his chair.

"Your intuition's right," he admitted. "I *was* sort of avoiding you."

"Hmm."

"If you recall," said Max, raising one eyebrow, "we exchanged a few choice words in your cabin."

Julie nodded. She remembered all too well. In fact, some of the things Max had said were still ringing in her ears.

"I was pretty steamed when I left there," he continued. "I was in no mood to sit at a table and make small talk, not with this Pierson-Roth business hanging over my head."

Julie gave a little wince.

"Don't take it personally, Julie," he said. "I realize that you're just the messenger."

"I hope you'll keep that in mind," she said.

"Well, anyway," said Max, "I decided to come over here to cool down and do some quiet thinking. I also needed to fire off an e-mail to Pierson-Roth. I wanted to ask them why no one had bothered to tell me that they were sending you down here." He grunted. "If someone's on a mission to twist my arm, I'd at least like some advance warning."

"I would too," admitted Julie. "So, what did you find out?"

"Oh, it was just an honest mistake," said Max, rubbing the back of his neck. "When I checked my e-mail tonight, I found an apology from the board member who was supposed to have told me about your visit. Turns out he was in bed all last week with the flu and was unable to take care of business." He shrugged. "So that explains that."

Julie nodded.

"Oh, and I got a message from Karen," said Max.

"The grad student from the University of Indiana," said Julie.

"Right," said Max. "Some kind of personal business has

come up—she didn't say what—and she's had to postpone her trip down here."

"Well," said Julie, "that's good news for me, isn't it? I won't have to move out of my cabin after all."

"I thought you were looking forward to sleeping in the dining hall," said Max, needling her in jest. "Aren't you the one who doesn't mind roughing it?"

"Oh, I prefer a bed over a hard floor any day," said Julie, laughing. She regarded Max, adding in a light manner, "Either way, you're stuck with me."

Max made a grumbling sound, but Julie could tell that the idea was not altogether repellent to him.

Just then, Julie remembered something Max had mentioned to her earlier that evening.

"Where's Lucy?" she asked, glancing around.

"You just missed her," said Max, amusement pulling at the corners of his mouth. "She was here a minute ago."

"I still think you're making this up," said Julie. "There's no one named Lucy residing in the lounge."

"You're going to eat those words," said Max, wagging a finger at her. "Watch this."

He searched his dinner plate and found a tiny piece of chicken. He picked up the morsel and carefully placed it on a ledge running along the back wall. Then he tapped on the ledge and returned to his seat.

"Be very still," he said, glancing at Julie, "and keep your eyes on that chicken."

"But why?" said Julie, feeling silly. She was sure that Max was pulling a prank on her. "There's no one else here. It's just you and me and those geckos over there."

"Shh," said Max, putting a finger to his lips. "Now, just be patient and watch."

Julie suppressed the urge to roll her eyes, and then she stared at the ledge as instructed. A minute went by during which nothing happened.

Then Julie caught her breath as a big tarantula squeezed through a crack in the wall and crawled onto the ledge. The tarantula delicately sidled over to claim the piece of chicken, and then vanished with it back into its lair.

"Wow," said Julie, letting out her breath, "so that's Lucy." She laughed. "That's the biggest spider I've ever seen."

"Yep," said Max, "that's Lucy. She's been living behind that wall for a couple of years now. She and the geckos keep the insects in check, but Lucy obviously also likes chicken." He gave Julie a teasing smile. "Now, aren't you sorry you doubted me?"

"Yes, I am," said Julie, laughing again. She placed a hand over her heart in a gesture of mock contrition. "Please forgive me, oh lord of the jungle. I'll never challenge your word again." She glanced at the crack in the wall. "Lucy's the first tarantula I've ever seen in the wild."

"What do you think of her?" asked Max.

"I've never been a big fan of spiders," admitted Julie, "but Lucy's beautiful. I'll have to come back here sometime and sketch her."

"Bring some chicken," said Max.

Julie chuckled, and then she said, "What an amazing day this has been."

"How so?" said Max, curiosity written on his face.

"I can't believe," said Julie, "how many first-time experiences I've had."

"Hmm, let's see," said Max, and began ticking things off on his fingers. "You got lost in the rain forest." There was a twinkle in his eye. "That had to be a first."

"Don't remind me," said Julie, wincing a little.

"You saw your first morpho butterfly," continued Max.

"As well as my first gecko," said Julie, "and my first tarantula." She regarded him. "And don't forget the hummingbird."

"Oh, yeah," said Max, nodding, "that was your first blue-tailed emerald." He paused for a heartbeat or two and locked eyes with Julie. "I see you're still wearing the flower."

"Oh, this," said Julie, touching the blossom with her fingers. "I'd forgotten it was there." She gave a self-conscious laugh. "Actually, this is a different one. I picked it right before I came in here."

"Really," said Max, with a thoughtful expression on his handsome face. A spark of interest kindled in his eyes.

Julie felt a flush creeping up her neck. What must Max think, that she was flirting with him by adorning herself with flowers?

But it was true. She *was* flirting with him. She knew that and now he probably knew it too. Her impulse to tuck another flower in her hair had sprung from a desire to have Max notice her. Not as an adversary but as a woman.

Julie suddenly felt naked, with her innermost thoughts exposed, and her flush deepened. She quickly changed the subject.

"So, what are you working on?" she asked, nodding toward the pile of papers and file folders on the table. "If you don't mind my asking."

Max pulled his eyes away from Julie. He cleared his throat.

"I'm, uh, writing a field guide to the birds of Manu National Park," he said. "Here, I'll show you."

He brought out a map of the Upper Amazon Basin. The two of them leaned forward to look at the map, their heads almost touching.

Julie was so distracted by Max's nearness that she could barely keep her mind on business.

"My book will include this whole area," said Max, tracing a large section with his finger.

"That's a big project," said Julie. "You have a lot of ground to cover."

"Most of the fieldwork has already been done," explained Max. "My job is to sift through the data that's been collected by me and others, and then write the text for each species." He nodded toward his laptop. "That's what I was doing when you came in."

"Will your field guide include *all* the birds in the park?" asked Julie.

"Every last one of them," said Max.

"But how can you be sure?" said Julie, out of curiosity. "Didn't I read somewhere that new species sometimes pop up in the rain forest?"

"Undiscovered species do show up now and then," said Max, "but this area has been so thoroughly studied that I doubt we'll find anything new." He shrugged. "It can happen, but it's a long shot."

"I see," said Julie.

"I've got the text three-quarters written," said Max, "but I'm no artist." He rubbed the side of his jaw. "I still have to find someone who can paint the color plates."

"You mean," said Julie, "pictures of the birds?"

"That's right," said Max. "Field guides need to have both a written description and an accurate picture of each species."

"Hmm," said Julie, as the seed of an idea germinated in her mind.

"This is where we are, by the way," said Max, indicating a spot on the map.

"What's this?" asked Julie, pointing to another place located downriver on a tributary that fed into the Manu River.

"That's the village of Laguna Miguel," said Max. "It's just inside the park boundary. Some of our workers come from there."

"How far is Laguna Miguel from here?" said Julie.

"Not far," said Max. "It takes about an hour by boat. It's a colorful little place."

"It sounds interesting," said Julie. She kept her voice neutral. "Any chance you could run me down there sometime?"

"It's doubtful," said Max, shaking his head. "I do have a research station to run, you know. I'm pretty busy, but you can hitch a ride with Cesar. His grandmother lives in Laguna Miguel. He goes down to check on her every week."

"I see," murmured Julie, trying not to show her disappointment that Max would not be her guide instead.

She changed the subject.

"Max," she said, "I've been thinking about the report I have to write for Pierson-Roth."

"What about it?" said Max, his jaw tensing.

"I was hoping you'd let me shadow you for a few days," she said, and held her breath. Would Max agree to such an arrangement?

"Shadow me?" said Max. He leaned back in his chair and folded his hands in his lap.

"I want to learn all I can about Manu River," said Julie, hoping to persuade him. "What better place to start than with the director and his duties?" She paused. "So, how about it?"

"Are you kidding?" said Max, with a sound of mild derision. "You wouldn't be able to keep up with me."

"What are you talking about?" said Julie. "Of course I can keep up."

Was Max speaking literally? Julie remembered the brisk pace he'd set on the forest path. She'd been forced to run a few steps now and then to make up for Max's long strides.

"Set whatever pace you want," she said, giving a nonchalant shrug. "I'll keep up."

"I doubt it," said Max, sounding as if his mind were made up. "Besides," he added, "why would I want someone from Pierson-Roth tagging along with me all day? We'd only get on each other's nerves." He lowered his brows. "Are you forgetting that we're on opposite sides of the Foundation's *brilliant* plan to bring tourists to Manu River?"

"Of course not," said Julie, "but that's exactly why I want to shadow you. I need to get a clear sense of your job here, Max, because it will have a bearing on my recommendations."

"Well, *my* recommendation," said Max, beginning to show

some irritation, "is that you gather information on your own. If you were to follow me around, I can just imagine us constantly butting heads over the issue." He blew out his breath. "No, Julie, I'd rather you didn't shadow me."

"I promise not to slow you down or get in your way," said Julie, "and I'll try not to say anything that will antagonize you."

Max said nothing.

Julie tried another tack. "You want my report to be fair, don't you?"

"Well, of course, I do," said Max, with an impatient gesture, "but—"

"I was sent here to do a job," said Julie. "You said you'd cooperate with me, so let me shadow you."

There was a long silence. Max stared at the ceiling. He glowered, but he also seemed to be giving Julie's proposal due consideration.

"I've got a long list of things to do tomorrow," he finally said. "The pace might be grueling." He regarded her. "Are you sure about this?"

"Try me," said Julie, raising her chin.

Max nodded. "All right," he said, "you're on. I'll pick you up at your cabin in the morning. Be ready for a very full day, beginning with a trek into the forest. Wear boots and bring a flashlight."

"A flashlight?"

"Yep," said Max, "we're leaving at five o'clock."

"But that's before sunrise," said Julie, with a little frown of surprise. "We're leaving in the dark?"

"Which is why you'll need a flashlight," said Max. "Unless that's too early for you," he added, making an expansive gesture with his hands. "I mean if you'd rather sleep in, I'm happy to go on my own. I was planning to anyway."

Julie was silent.

"You could stay behind and have a leisurely breakfast," continued Max. "If you ask him nicely, Hernando might even serve it to you in bed."

"Okay, you've made your point," said Julie, glaring at him. "You're just trying to scare me off. But guess what? I'm not going to let you."

She stood up to leave.

"I'll be ready at five o'clock," she said, and gave a bright smile. "I look forward to it."

Julie was carefully hiding her true feelings. She hated the thought of dragging herself out of bed before the sun was up. And plunging into the jungle in the dark had no appeal at all. She was dreading the next day, but she wouldn't dream of letting Max know that.

Just then, she remembered something. "I may need this," she said. Reaching out, she whipped her bandanna from Max's vest pocket. "Good night."

The irritating sound of Max's soft laughter followed her to the door.

Chapter Five

The sound of someone knocking at her door jolted Julie awake before dawn the next morning. She sat up in bed with a start, feeling confused and disoriented in the total darkness of her cabin.

The knocking came again, louder this time.

"Who is it?" she called.

"It's Max," rumbled a voice, from outside. "It's five o'clock. Are you ready to go?"

"Five o'clock?" said Julie. Her heart began to race. "It can't be."

She rubbed the sleep from her eyes and picked up her travel clock from the bedside table. The clock's luminous dial confirmed that it was, indeed, five o'clock in the morning. She'd intended for the alarm to awaken her at 4:45, but it must not have gone off.

Checking the back of the clock with her fingers, Julie discovered the problem.

"Darn it," she said, muttering to herself. Then she called, "Max?"

"What?"

"I was so tired last night," she said, "I guess I forgot to pull out the alarm button on my travel clock. Sorry."

There was a short pause.

"That's okay," said Max. "Go back to sleep. I'll catch you another time."

Julie heard the sound of Max turning around on the porch and then walking down the steps. He was leaving without her.

"No, wait!" she cried, and jumped out of bed. "It'll only take me a minute to get ready."

"I don't have time to wait around," said Max. "I need to be at the canopy platform before the sun comes up."

"Canopy platform?" said Julie, frantically feeling around in the dark for her clothes. "That sounds interesting. Is it up in the treetops?"

"Yes."

"Well, just give me a couple of minutes, okay?"

She heard Max exhale with impatience and say something under his breath.

"Please?" she added, stripping off her nightclothes and tossing them aside.

"Okay," said Max, sounding none too happy about the situation, "but hurry up, will you?"

"I'm hurrying," said Julie.

She considered lighting a candle to illuminate the room, but she couldn't remember where the candles and matches were located. Besides, there were no curtains on the screened windows. For the sake of modesty, Julie decided to dress in the dark.

But that was easier said than done. She couldn't locate her bra, so she put on a tank top without it. Then she tossed on a long-sleeved shirt and some long pants. Next, she pulled on a pair of socks, jammed her feet into her boots, and fumbled with the laces.

Once she was dressed, Julie used her flashlight to light her way to the bathroom. She quickly used the toilet, brushed her teeth, and splashed water in her face, trying to wake up.

Julie's mind was racing. The sun wasn't even up yet and, thanks to her, the day was already starting off on the wrong foot. She chided herself for not having double-checked her alarm clock the night before. She'd overslept because of a careless mistake, and now Max was going to think that she was disorganized and scatterbrained.

Oh, well, she thought, with spirit, *let him think what he likes.*

"Julie," called Max, "what's keeping you?"

"I'm coming," she answered.

She grabbed her knapsack and headed for the door.

"Thanks for waiting, Max," she said, as she joined him on the boardwalk.

Julie looked around. The camp was drenched in darkness. The lanterns along the boardwalk had been extinguished, and Julie and Max's flashlights were the only sources of illumination. Everything was still and silent. The air was cool and refreshing, with the rich smell of plants and damp earth.

Julie breathed deeply, filling her lungs with the spicy-sweet essence of the rain forest. She craved a hot cup of coffee. But she'd have to make do with fresh air and exercise to sweep the lingering cobwebs of sleepiness from her brain.

"Good morning," she said, doing her best to sound awake and chipper. "That is, if you can call the inky blackness of midnight morning," she added, tossing out a bit of humor.

"Come on," said Max, turning to go. "We're already late."

"Gee, it's nice to see you too," said Julie, muttering under her breath.

"Excuse me?" said Max.

"Oh, nothing," said Julie. "I was just thinking what fun it is to be up with the chickens. Or should I say the parrots?" She paused. "Do you always get up this early?"

"No," said Max, "but there's a reason for it this morning."

"Which is?"

"You'll see when we get there."

"Hmm."

"This was your idea, remember," said Max. "You were determined to tag along with me. No one's forcing you to go." He shrugged. "So if you'd rather stay here—"

"Oh, no," said Julie, with a show of spirit, "you can't get rid of me that easily." Max was testing her resolve and she knew it. "You're stuck with me, Mister Science."

"Feeling spunky, are we?" said Max, chuckling.

"I'd feel a lot spunkier," said Julie, pretending to grumble, "if I'd had a cup of coffee." She stifled a yawn.

"I've got a thermos right in here," said Max, patting his bulging daypack.

"You brought coffee?" said Julie. She was both surprised and impressed.

"And two cups," said Max. "We'll have some at the canopy platform. Can you wait until then?"

"Yes, I can wait," said Julie, suddenly feeling as happy as a kid on a field trip. She put on her knapsack and adjusted the straps. "Lead on to the canopy platform."

"All right, follow me," said Max, as he began striding along the boardwalk.

Julie fell in behind him. Noticing how the twin beams of their flashlights marked the way like two friends, she felt a shiver of excitement. She was heading off into the rain forest with the most attractive and fascinating man she'd ever met. She couldn't guess what lay ahead, but she knew that the day was bound to be an adventure.

"Okay, here we are," said Max.

He and Julie had walked along a forest path for half an hour. Now they stopped at a giant rain forest tree. Max shined his light on the tree, showing Julie an iron ladder solidly anchored to the trunk. The ladder scaled the trunk and disappeared into the branches high above.

"Where's the platform?" asked Julie.

"It's way up there," said Max, pointing over their heads. "You can't see it from down here, because it's still dark. When you get up there, you'll feel like you're on top of the world."

"Wait a minute," said Julie, her mouth going dry. "Are you saying that we have to climb this ladder?"

"That's right."

"Uh, I don't know about this," she said, hesitating.

"Are you afraid of heights?" said Max.

"Not usually."

"Well, what is it, then?"

"I've just never done anything like this before," said Julie, with a nervous laugh. "I've climbed a step ladder to change a lightbulb, but nothing this daring." She wiped her palms on her pant legs. "When I said I wanted to shadow you, I didn't picture scaling a tall tree in the middle of the night."

"Trust me," said Max, "you're going to like it up there. This ladder's perfectly safe. All you have to do is hang on, take your time, and place your feet carefully on each rung." He regarded her. "Of course, you don't have to go. You can stay here and wait for me."

"Oh, no," said Julie, shaking her head and glancing around at the dark, mysterious forest. "I'm not staying down here by myself." She swallowed. "If you're going, I'm going. Besides, I want that cup of coffee you mentioned."

"I can leave the coffee here with you," offered Max.

"No, I'm going," said Julie, screwing up her courage.

"That's the spirit," said Max.

"What have I gotten myself into?" said Julie, groaning to herself. She spoke to Max. "What's next on our list today, bungee jumping?"

Max laughed. Then he took off his pack and set it on the ground. He dug around in it and brought out a couple of headlamps.

"You'll need both hands for climbing," he explained, "so wear one of these."

Julie clicked off her flashlight and put it in her pocket. Then she let Max slip the elastic band of one of the lamps around her head. Max adjusted the band to give her a comfortable fit, with the light situated on her forehead.

"How's that feel?" he said, his hand briefly resting on Julie's shoulder.

"Fine," said Julie, trying to keep her mind on business. Max's touch was so distracting.

Max donned the other headlamp. Then he put on his pack and buckled the waist strap.

"Okay, I think we're ready," he said, and showed Julie how to turn on her lamp. "You'll go first."

"Why me?"

"It's for safety," he said. "If you lose your footing, I'll be able to steady you." He gave her a little nudge toward the ladder. "Don't worry, I'll be right below you."

"Are you sure about this?" said Julie, taking hold of the ladder. The metal felt cool and solid in her hands.

"Students have been climbing this ladder for years," said Max. "No one's ever fallen or gotten hurt." He cast his eyes skyward. "Let's get going. We need to be on the platform before sunrise."

Julie took a deep breath, put her foot on the bottom rung, and began to climb.

"Take each step carefully," said Max. He put a reassuring hand on her ankle. "Remember, safety first."

They climbed in silence for a minute or two. Although Julie's heart was pounding, she knew that it was more from excitement than from fear. The events of the previous year had forced her to dig deeply for inner strength. As a result, she'd gained perspective and some valuable lessons along the way. Most surprising of all was learning that she could do things she'd never before thought possible.

Coping with Simon's death had been her first challenge, and then other challenges had quickly followed. When compared with what she'd had to deal with, climbing a ladder in a dark rain forest was a piece of cake.

"How's it going?" said Max, his voice breaking in on Julie's thoughts.

"This isn't so bad," said Julie, feeling a spurt of confidence. "In fact, I'm kind of enjoying it."

Just then, one of her feet slipped and she cried out. Before she knew what was happening, she felt Max's strong hand on the back of her thigh, holding her steady while she regained her footing.

"Are you okay?" he asked.

"Yes, I'm fine," said Julie, catching her breath.

She was keenly aware of the intimate pressure of Max's warm hand on her thigh. It was a strictly practical move on his part, to assure Julie's safety. Even so, his touch thrilled her.

"Thanks for the help," she added.

As Julie resumed climbing, she realized for the second time how safe she felt with Max. She knew that he would not let her fall, but there was more to her insight than that. Julie sensed a deep inner strength in Max's character. He was a rock a woman could lean on, a safe harbor in stormy weather.

Julie also knew that, however well she'd coped on her own in the past year, life's challenges were easier to face when one had a loving partner with whom to share the journey. Her heart squeezed with yearning. She'd been alone too long.

Presently, Julie reached a wooden platform near the top of the tree. She climbed the last two rungs of the ladder and stepped onto the platform, with Max right behind her.

Julie set down her knapsack and shined her light around. The solidly built platform spanned three enormous horizontal branches of the tree. There was a safety railing all around and two wooden benches.

"This takes me back to my childhood," said Julie, turning

to Max. "My brother and I had a tree house in our backyard, but this is much more impressive."

"There's room up here for ten people," said Max. He patted the trunk of the tree. "This big guy is as solid as they come." He regarded Julie. "Now, how about some coffee?"

"I'd love some," said Julie, feeling like a pampered princess on an exotic expedition.

Max took off his pack and brought out a thermos and two cups. As he poured the hot coffee, steam rose in the air. He handed a cup to Julie, and then they sat side by side on one of the benches.

"Now we need to douse our lights," said Max, removing his headlamp and turning it off, "and be as quiet as possible."

"Are we waiting for something to happen?" asked Julie, removing her headlamp and turning off her light. She sipped her coffee in the dark, breathing deeply its rich aroma.

"As soon as the sun comes up," said Max, "you're going to see some wonderful things." Julie heard the smile in his voice.

They drank their coffee in silence for a minute or two, their arms now and then brushing against each other. The darkness enfolded them in its friendly embrace, and Julie realized that there was nowhere else on earth she'd rather be. She savored the companionable intimacy of the moment, and wished with all her heart that she'd met Max under different circumstances.

She turned to speak to him in a whisper.

"Why did you build this platform?" she asked. "Does it have any special purpose?"

"It gives us access to the upper layer of the forest," said Max, his whispering breath warm on Julie's cheek. "It's the only way to get up to where some of the birds are," he continued. "Many rain forest species spend their entire lives in the canopy and are too high up in the branches to study from the ground. Up here, ornithology students are at eye level with those birds. We can also study the plants and insects that live in the canopy. Botanists and entomologists learn a lot up here too."

"I see," Julie said, and took another swallow of coffee. "Hmm," she added.

"What?" said Max.

"I was just thinking," said Julie. "Wouldn't birders be attracted to a platform like this?"

"Of course," said Max. "Anyone interested in tropical birds wants to have access to the canopy." Julie felt him lean his head in her direction. "I can almost hear the wheels turning in your brain," he added, with a touch of irony. "Where's this conversation leading? I think I already know, but go ahead anyway. What's on your mind, Julie?"

"I was just thinking that you've got the basics here for a prime birding destination," said Julie. "Of course, you'd have to create a more accessible method for getting people up here." She thought for a moment. "How hard would it be to replace that iron ladder with, say, a set of steps with a handrail?"

"Not difficult at all," said Max, his arm grazing Julie's as he raised his cup to his lips. "My workers can build anything I ask them to. They're excellent carpenters." He paused. "But the ladder's good enough for scientific purposes. Why change it?"

"Because when visitors start coming here," said Julie, "you'll need to offer better access to this platform."

Max sighed. "I don't want visitors here," he said. "Besides, there are canopy platforms at some of the eco-lodges I've already mentioned. Birders can go to those."

There was a strained silence.

"You can't fight this," said Julie, speaking softly. "Tourists are going to come to Manu River, whether or not you approve of the plan." She laid her hand on his arm. "Please work with me, Max. I'm trying to be helpful."

"No, you're trying to ruin my morning," said Max, grumbling. "Can't we just sit here in peace and enjoy the forest?"

"We have to discuss the details sooner or later," said Julie. "Big changes are coming to Manu River, and the Foundation wants you to be a part of them."

Max said nothing.

"You're running out of money, Max," said Julie. "Tourism would keep Manu River open and its finances in the black."

"I'll find funding somewhere else," said Max.

"That's the Foundation's responsibility," said Julie. "You're a scientist with important work to do. Fundraising is a full-time job. You can't do your work and raise money too."

Suddenly Max surprised Julie by laughing softly.

"What's so funny?" said Julie, feeling a spurt of annoyance. How could Max laugh when she was trying to be serious?

Max leaned toward her in the dark, their shoulders touching. "Are you always this earnest before dawn?" he said, teasing her.

"I'm just trying to tell you—"

"Shh," he said, lightly laying his hand on her arm. "We're up here to see something very special, and we're going to ruin it with all this bickering."

"We have to talk about these things," said Julie.

"And we will," said Max, "but not now. Okay?"

"Okay," said Julie, letting out her breath.

She leaned back against the tree trunk, her mind in a whirl of frustration. She wanted to help Max. Why couldn't he see that?

A few minutes went by in silence. Then Max spoke.

"Here comes the sun," he whispered, as a hint of color appeared in the eastern sky. He leaned forward with an air of excited anticipation. "Heads up, Julie," he said. "You're about to see one of the best shows on Planet Earth."

As Julie and Max watched from their lofty perch, dawn broke in the rain forest. Shades of rose and flamingo-pink stained the sky, growing more intense and then fading to blue as the sun peeped over the horizon. The sun's rays warmed the air and bathed each tree, each leaf, and each wandering vine with a golden sheen.

Julie regarded Max, sitting close beside her. He turned his head and their eyes met. A silent message seemed to flow between the two of them. They were witnessing the birth of a new day in one of the most pristine environments on earth. The platform in the treetops gave them the perfect vantage point from which to view this miracle. They were on top of the world, surrounded by a sea of green.

"This is amazing," said Julie, whispering.

Max nodded and spoke softly. "So, was it worth it?" he asked. "Dragging yourself out of bed at five o'clock, I mean."

"Oh, yes," said Julie, in a voice of awe. "I've seen sunrises before, but nothing this magical."

She gazed around at the forest stretching as far as the eye could see. Some of the trees bore a mantle of brightly colored blossoms. From the crowns of other giants, condensation rose into the air as steam.

"Everything looks so beautiful and so primitive," she continued. She thought for a moment. "It feels as if we've gone way back in time, doesn't it? To the very beginning."

"Being in the rain forest," said Max, "is probably as close as you'll get to time travel. This is one of the oldest forests on earth," he added. "But the show's just beginning. Keep watching."

"And listening," said Julie. "Everything was so still and silent just a minute ago. Now I'm hearing all sorts of things. Birds and insects, water dripping on leaves, and—" She stopped suddenly and stared into the distance. "What on earth is that loud roaring sound?"

"Those are howler monkeys," said Max. "The big males give that booming call to announce their territory. It can be heard for miles."

Just then, a raucous chattering filled the air.

"Look!" cried Julie, pointing to half a dozen large birds flying past at eye level. The birds' brilliant plumage was a rainbow of red, yellow, and blue. She turned to Max with excitement.

"I've never seen wild parrots before," she said.

"They're in the parrot family," said Max, nodding. "Those

are scarlet macaws." He grinned at Julie. "Or *Ara macao,* if you prefer the scientific name."

Julie laughed. She was having the time of her life. And, from what she could tell, Max was enjoying himself as well. Her heart filled with gratitude. How glad she was that she and Max could put their differences aside to savor this moment.

They continued to watch as the rain forest stirred to life. Max pointed out various birds that flitted among the branches. There were toucans, odd little woodcreepers, and a handsome black-and-white magpie tanager.

Presently, Max refilled their cups with coffee and brought out a cloth bag.

"Could you eat something?" he said, reaching into the bag. "I've got breakfast."

"You brought food?" said Julie, suddenly realizing how hungry she was. "You've thought of everything."

"Well, it's nothing fancy," said Max, with a half smile, "but it'll hold us until lunch."

He handed Julie a banana, a hard-boiled egg, and some bread and butter wrapped in waxed paper.

"You've gone to a lot of trouble," said Julie, peeling her egg. "Because of me, you've had to bring extra food."

"So I had to boil two eggs instead of one," said Max, shrugging. "No big deal. Besides," he added, "I'm, uh, actually glad to have the company."

"Really?" said Julie, studying him.

"Sure," he said. "I don't mind working out here on my own, but it does get a bit lonely at times." He gazed out over the dawn-lit forest. "I also happen to believe that experiences like this are meant to be shared."

"I completely agree," said Julie, her heart expanding with contentment.

Max cleared his throat and busied himself with his food. Julie sensed that he'd revealed more than he'd intended.

"Oh, look," he said, presently, "here they are."

"Here *what* are?" said Julie, glancing around.

"You're going to love this," said Max, bringing out a camera with a telephoto lens. "This is the main reason why I wanted to be here so early. I need to get some pictures of these guys."

He walked to the railing. "Come over here, Julie," he called back to her. "You don't want to miss this."

Julie set her breakfast aside and joined Max at the railing.

"What are we looking for?" she asked.

"Just keep your eyes on that tall tree over there," said Max, adjusting his camera.

Following Max's instructions, Julie focused her attention on the tree he'd indicated. The leaves and branches rustled with movement, yet there was no wind. Now and then, she caught a flash of brown among the foliage, and she could hear the chattering of many voices.

"What are those?" she asked.

"Squirrel monkeys," said Max, beginning to take pictures. "About a hundred of them. They're hanging out in this part of the forest right now to eat the ripe fruit on those fig trees over there."

He nodded toward some trees that stood on the edge of an open space. His camera whirred.

"Heads up!" he said. "There they go!"

As Julie watched, the squirrel monkeys began leaping across the open space in a downward plummet that carried them to the fig trees below. For a few moments, it "rained" squirrel monkeys as more and more of them jumped the gap, emboldened by the promise of sweet figs on the other side. The sunshine burnished their fur with highlights, turning the stream of monkeys into a golden waterfall.

"This is amazing," said Julie, enchanted by the sight of a hundred monkeys leaping through the air like daredevils. "I've seen squirrel monkeys in zoos, but seeing them in the wild is ten times better." She watched in awe. "I can hardly believe my eyes."

When the last monkey had crossed the open space, the tribe settled down to plunder the ripe fruit. Julie and Max returned to the bench to finish their breakfast.

"You seemed to really enjoy those monkeys," said Max later, as they were putting things away.

"That was an incredible sight," said Julie. "Did you see the tiny babies clinging to their mothers?"

Max nodded.

"What a wild ride that must be," said Julie, laughing.

There was a long pause.

"Max?" said Julie.

"Yes?"

"I— I just want to tell you something," she began, searching for the right words. "I haven't felt this happy in a very long time." She looked at him. "So I just want to thank you."

"Don't thank me," said Max. "Thank the rain forest."

Although it sounded as if Max were brushing aside Julie's comment, she could tell that her words had touched him.

Julie nodded and looked down at her lap. She twisted her wedding band, unable to speak over the lump forming in her throat. Her emotions these days were never far from the surface.

Max reached over and covered her hand with his, as if he sensed her thoughts.

"You've had a pretty rough year, haven't you?" he said.

Again she mutely nodded.

"How'd your husband die?" said Max, in a kindly voice. "Do you want to talk about it?"

Julie swallowed. "Simon died in a kayaking accident in eastern Washington," she said. "He was competing in a race down the Wenatchee River." She blinked back some tears and composed herself before going on. "He'd had asthma his whole life.

He apparently had an asthma attack while he was racing, and then he lost control of his boat and drowned."

"Hmm," said Max.

He kept his hand on Julie's. It was a warm, strong presence that gave her confidence. She felt she could tell Max anything.

"It was all so sudden," said Julie, finally looking up. "I was at home in Seattle at the time. Simon had called me the morning of the race. I'd wished him luck, and then, by afternoon, he was gone." She bit her lip. "Just like that."

Max squeezed her hand. "That must have been terrible for you," he said.

"It's the worst thing that's ever happened to me," said Julie. She mused for a moment. "Life can certainly change in the blink of an eye, can't it?"

"Yes, it can," said Max, a note of personal sorrow entering his voice. He cleared his throat. "So, you must really miss him," he added.

"I do," said Julie. "We started dating in high school. Simon was my best friend." Her voice caught. "I could tell him anything."

There was a long, thoughtful silence. Max finally spoke.

"You know what I think?" he said.

"What?" asked Julie, turning to look into his eyes. What she saw reflected in their blue depths was a mixture of compassion and yearning.

"I think your husband," said Max, "was one lucky guy. No one has ever loved me the way you obviously loved him."

"But, Max," said Julie, her heart reaching out to him, "you were married."

"Being married," said Max, with a touch of irony, "doesn't guarantee the kind of relationship you had with your husband." He shook his head and sighed. "Barbara and I were certainly in love when we married—or at least I thought we were—but all of that changed."

"What happened?" said Julie. "I mean, if you care to talk about it."

"To put it bluntly," said Max, "she had an affair with someone in her office."

"Oh no," said Julie, trying to imagine how anyone could betray a partner's trust in such a devastating manner.

"I never met the guy, which is probably a good thing," said Max. He gave a rough laugh. "At the time, I'm sure I would've punched his lights out." Then he rubbed his chin with the back of his hand. "But now I realize that I actually owe the guy a thank-you."

"What do you mean?" said Julie.

"Well, he did me a favor," said Max. "He helped me see that Barbara and I weren't a good fit and never were. What she really wanted, as it turns out, was a buttoned-down nine-to-fiver who stayed close to home, not a scientist who spends six months a year in the rain forest."

"I see."

"Now she's got what she wants," said Max. "She married the guy and they're expecting their first child." He regarded Julie. "I was pretty torn up at the time, but I can say now that I wish them all the best." He nodded. "I honestly do."

"That's generous of you," said Julie, not sure what else to say.

"Well, what can you do?" said Max, gesturing with his hand. "What happened, happened, and, well, I guess I've chalked it up to experience."

"Do you still have feelings for her?" asked Julie, softly.

"Oh, no," said Max, with quiet emphasis. "That's all behind me."

"Hmm."

"What about you?" said Max, studying Julie's face.

"Well," said Julie, searching for the right words, "Simon will always have a place in my heart, but—" She hesitated.

"But what?" said Max.

"I know that he'd want me to move on," said Julie, feeling a mix of bittersweet emotions at the admission. "I couldn't have said that a couple of months ago, but now I can." She glanced down at her wedding band. "Simon wouldn't want me to be alone for the rest of my life. He'd want me to find someone else. I'm sure of that."

"Hmm."

Max gently withdrew his hand from on top of Julie's and stared into the distance for a few moments. He seemed lost in thought.

"You know," he said, turning back to her, "I've been meaning to ask you something. How'd you get mixed up with Pierson-Roth?"

"The answer to that," said Julie, "is kind of complicated."

"I'm listening," said Max. He crossed his arms across his chest and leaned back against the tree trunk.

"Right after Simon died," said Julie, "the door-manufacturing company I worked for was forced to downsize." She shrugged. "With fewer houses being built these days, the demand for doors is way down, and I suddenly found myself out of a job."

"So you lost your husband *and* your job?" said Max.

"Yes."

"That must have been tough," said Max. "How'd you get through two major blows at once?"

"Not very well, at first," she admitted.

"What happened?"

"I kind of retreated from life," she said, remembering the several weeks she'd spent in grief and withdrawal. "I took long walks, I watched old movies, and I cried a lot."

She exhaled.

"Then I woke up one morning," she went on, "and realized that I was feeling a little better. A few days later, I pulled myself together and started looking for another job."

"And that's when you signed on with Pierson-Roth?" said Max.

"No," said Julie, shaking her head. "I was actually working at a bookstore when I heard about the opening at Pierson-Roth."

"Why'd you switch over to them?" said Max, with a little frown.

"The pay was better," said Julie, "but that's not the main reason I changed jobs." She gave a little laugh, suddenly feeling self-conscious. "You know, I haven't told this to anyone. You may not believe me."

"Try me," said Max.

Julie studied his face for a moment, suddenly wondering how far she could trust Max with some of her most private feelings. How would he react when he learned the truth about her motives for hiring on with Pierson-Roth?

Julie decided to take a chance on him.

"I went to work for Pierson-Roth," she said, taking a deep breath, "because someone dared me to."

Chapter Six

Y ou applied for a job at Pierson-Roth on a dare?" said Max, staring at Julie in disbelief. "What are you talking about?"

"I know," said Julie, with a self-conscious shake of her head, "it sounds strange, doesn't it?"

She glanced out at the forest surrounding the canopy platform. The rising sun was glazing the leaves with light, and the air was growing warmer and more humid. She unfastened the top buttons of her long-sleeved shirt and fanned herself with her hand.

"Oh, it's more than strange," said Max, his jaw tightening. "Excuse me, because I know you must have had your reasons, but to take a job on a dare sounds frivolous and impulsive and—"

"But you haven't heard the whole story," said Julie, dismayed by Max's response. Tension rippled in the air, replacing the mood of tranquility that had marked the morning.

"It had better be good," said Max, frowning. "Because I'm having trouble accepting that someone on a *dare* has come down here to pressure me on behalf of Pierson-Roth."

"Are you going to allow me to explain?" said Julie, with a spurt of annoyance. "Or would you rather continue ranting?"

Max said nothing. By way of response, he simply gave an impatient go-ahead-I'm-listening wave of his hand.

"Yes," said Julie, taking a calming breath, "I applied for the opening at Pierson-Roth on a dare. But my reasons certainly weren't frivolous or impulsive. There's a lot more to the story."

"Go on."

"I need to back up a bit," said Julie, "and tell you about my Army cousin Bethany. A few months ago, she was completing her second tour in Iraq, when her convoy was ambushed." Julie regarded Max. "She survived the attack, but she lost a leg."

"I'm sorry to hear that," said Max, his demeanor thawing into a look of compassion. "Losing a limb must be tough."

"Yes, it's been challenging for her," said Julie, "because she's always been fit and active." Then she smiled. "But you don't know my cousin. She's one of the most positive people I've ever met. She'd never let life get the better of her."

Max nodded.

"When I went to see her in rehab," continued Julie, "she was being fitted for a prosthesis." She regarded Max. "She was incredibly grateful to be alive. And do you know what she told me?"

"What?"

"She said she's planning to run a half-marathon next year," said Julie. She gave an affectionate laugh. "Knowing Bethany, she'll probably do it too."

"Wow, good for her," said Max.

"Yes, good for her," said Julie. "I plan to be there, cheering her on. Even if she has to walk the last couple of miles, I know she'll reach the finish line."

There was a reflective pause. As the sun rose higher, its rays filtered through the leaves and fell on Julie and Max's shoulders.

"So, um, back to the dare," said Max, waving an insect away from his face. "Where does that fit in?"

"When Bethany heard that I was working in a bookstore," said Julie, "she told me that I'd taken the easy way out."

"What did she mean by that?" said Max.

"She meant that in light of all I'd been through," said Julie, "I was due for a big change. I'd lost my husband. I'd lost my job. According to Bethany, I was just marking time at the bookstore."

"Is that how you felt?" said Max, studying her. "As if you were just marking time?"

"Not at first," said Julie, shaking her head. "Considering what had happened, my job at the bookstore served a purpose. It let me ease back into the human race, if that makes sense."

"Hmm."

"It wasn't a very demanding position," she continued, "and the nine-to-five routine suited me. But I was growing restless. I knew there was something different out there for me, something that would truly engage my interest." She shrugged. "I wanted to feel passionate about something again. I just didn't know what that something was yet."

"Go on."

"When Bethany challenged me to get out there and take more risks," said Julie, "I knew she was on the right track."

She regarded Max.

"My cousin really inspired me," she went on. "I told myself that if she could lose a leg and still have a positive outlook on life, I should be able to rise to the occasion too. All that was holding me back were my own doubts and fears."

Max nodded.

"Then something came along," said Julie, "that forced me to take some action."

"What happened?" said Max, listening.

"I got the proverbial kick in the rear," said Julie, with a rueful laugh. "One day while I was at work, my apartment building burned down."

Max frowned and gave a low whistle.

"Fortunately, no one was injured," said Julie, "but I lost everything."

She paused, remembering the shock of coming home to a scene of total destruction. In her mind's eye, she could still see the smoke rising from the rubble and smell the pungent odor of charred wood and crumbled masonry.

"It was all gone," she continued. "Furniture, clothing, some framed art I really loved, a rug my mom had made just a year before she died . . . everything was gone."

She sighed.

"Worst of all," she added, "my entire history with Simon had gone up in flames. I wasn't able to salvage even one photograph—not of him, not of us together, nothing." She shook her head. "I can replace most of the other stuff, but losing all of my pictures was really hard."

There was another thoughtful silence.

"You are one tough woman," said Max. He regarded Julie with a look of admiration.

"Do you really think so?" said Julie, encouraged by his words.

"Of course I do," said Max. "I never would've guessed that you'd been through all that in the past year."

"The stronger the wind, the stronger the tree," said Julie, musing quietly as she watched a handsome forest hawk glide past. "That was a quote in a card that Bethany sent to me right after the fire."

"Hmm."

"When I got that card," said Julie, "I decided that the fire had given me a wonderful opportunity. It gave me a kind of freedom I hadn't had before." She glanced at Max. "Does that make sense?"

"I think so," said Max. "Go on."

"As terrible as it was to lose all of my possessions and keepsakes, I came to realize that the fire had wiped the slate clean, in a manner of speaking."

Max nodded.

"I had nothing more to lose," explained Julie, "and there was nothing holding me back. I was a widow with nowhere to live and nothing but the clothes on my back, and I was working at a job I didn't really care about. It was time for a change. I could head off in an entirely different direction, if I wanted to." She smiled. "It was a scary thought, but it was exciting too."

"Yes, I can imagine that," said Max.

"When I went to see Bethany after the fire," said Julie, "I told her that I'd heard about an opening at the Pierson-Roth Foundation. The job involved a visit to the rain forest."

She laughed.

"I'd never been farther away from home than northern California," she went on. "Traveling to the Upper Amazon Basin sounded like going to the moon. I was scared and nervous. I didn't know what to expect, and, to be honest, I almost didn't apply."

"And then Bethany dared you to do it," said Max.

"That's right," said Julie. "Bethany looked me straight in the eye and said that if I didn't apply for that job, I'd always regret it." She glanced over at Max. "So I did and, well, here I am."

"Yes, here you are," said Max. Then he added, with a self-deprecating smile, "I suppose I owe you an apology. Your reasons for taking this job were anything but frivolous. I'm sorry I jumped to conclusions about your motives." He rubbed his chin. "Guess I'm a little touchy these days on the subject of Pierson-Roth."

"Apology accepted," said Julie, smiling. "In your shoes, I'd probably be touchy too."

"Well, anyway," continued Max, "it took guts to apply for a new job and travel all the way to South America. I'd call that a leap of faith."

"Sort of like those squirrel monkeys," said Julie, laughing. She glanced down at the fig trees where the monkeys were still feasting among the branches.

"Yeah," said Max, slanting her a smile, "you could say that."

As she watched the monkeys, Julie mused that their leap of faith had paid off in a banquet of sweet fruit. Would Julie's leap of faith bring rewards to her as well?

Her heart expanded as she gave a sidelong glance in Max's direction. She tried to read his profile. Anything was possible, wasn't it?

"I believe in giving credit where it's due," said Max, his voice breaking in on her thoughts. He brushed some dust from his pant leg. "It's a shame we're on opposite teams, so to speak, but I salute you all the same."

"Why must we define ourselves as opponents?" said Julie, with a little frown.

"Because that's what we are," said Max, raising one brow.

"But it sounds so unfriendly," said Julie, feeling anything but unfriendly toward Max at the moment.

"We can dance around the situation any way you like," said Max, shrugging, "but the fact remains that you and I are not on the same team."

"We could say that, I suppose," said Julie, conceding the point, "but I believe we can work together. I'm here to help, if you'll let me."

"But I hate the basic plan," said Max, grumbling. "I can't imagine how the Foundation thinks it'll work."

"Maybe this will persuade you," said Julie, reaching into her knapsack. "I brought something for you to look at." She handed Max a large brown envelope.

"What's this?" said Max, eyeing the envelope with suspicion. He pulled out some papers.

"These are financial spreadsheets from the Foundation," explained Julie. "They cover the last three years, up to the present."

"I've already seen this stuff," said Max, dismissing the papers with a wave of his hand. "This material was published in Pierson-Roth's annual report."

"Not this most recent data," said Julie, indicating the last sheet in the pile. "The Foundation's accountant ran this off for me right before I came down here." She held up the paper. "Take a good look, Max."

There was silence on the platform as Max bent his head over the papers and studied them. He riffled through the pile, each time coming back to the most recent spreadsheet. When he finally looked up, grim lines etched his face.

"Things are worse than I thought," he said, his voice heavy with disappointment. "Are you sure about these figures? They can't be right."

"They're accurate," said Julie, her heart going out to him. She hated having to share such discouraging news. "I'm sorry, Max," she went on, "but as you can plainly see, there's just not enough money coming in right now. The board had to scramble for funds last year, and now things are even worse."

"It looks like we've lost some of our biggest donors," he said, in a dull voice. He glanced back through the spreadsheets.

"That's right," said Julie, nodding. "The economy's been soft lately, and, well, this is one of the results."

"Hmm," said Max, compressing his lips.

"I wish I had better news," said Julie, "but there you have it." She studied his profile. "Manu River is running out of money. It's that simple."

Max gave a silent nod and then replaced the sheets in the envelope. He handed the envelope to Julie, and she put it back into her knapsack.

Max murmured something under his breath.

"I'm sorry?" said Julie.

"The stronger the wind, the stronger the tree," repeated Max, leveling his gaze at Julie. "It's a good thought. I like it." There was a glint of determination in his eyes. "I will find a way to get through this," he declared, making a fist and thumping his knee. "There must be a way."

"As you know," said Julie, choosing her words with care, "the solution to Manu River's money woes is already in the works. The only way the research station can carry on is to bring in ecotourists."

She leaned toward Max, hoping to reason with him.

"I'm talking about paying guests," she added, "with money to spend. Think what that could mean for Manu River."

"I've thought of little else," said Max, with a humorless laugh, "since hearing about it." A fierce expression crossed his face. "But I'd rather beg on a street corner," he said, with passion, "than change Manu River's mission. We've always been about *science,* Julie. You will never convince me that mingling research with tourism is a good idea."

There was a long, uncomfortable silence. The heat of mid-morning bore down on the platform. Julie unfastened the remaining buttons on her shirt and opened the front, allowing air to circulate around her bare neck and tank top. She turned to Max.

"What would you say," she began, dreading what she had to tell him, "if I told you that the Foundation has prepared a list of potential candidates to replace you as the director at Manu River?"

"I'd call that professional blackmail," said Max, his face darkening with anger. "They're telling me to play ball or get out." His eyes blazed. "Is that it?"

"Not in so many words," said Julie, aware that she was walking a fine line. "But try to see things from their perspective. They have to be practical. I've already told you that they want you to continue as director. They have no wish to find someone else."

"And yet they're already lining up people to replace me?" said Max, glowering into the distance.

"They're not lining up anybody," said Julie. "They've made a list, that's all. You can't really blame them. They have to keep all options open. If you don't want to oversee a transition that brings ecotourism to Manu River, they'll be forced to find someone else. And if that doesn't work, well, they'll have to close Manu River altogether."

"I can't believe this is happening," said Max, staring out at the lush rain forest he loved so much. "There has to be a better way." He paused, his forehead creased in thought. "Maybe I can—"

Before Max could finish his thought, Julie gave a startled cry and jumped to her feet.

"What's the matter?" said Max. He stood up as well.

"Something just flew under my shirt," said Julie.

She began flapping the sides of her open shirt, hoping that the insect would fly back out.

"What was it?" said Max, trying to be helpful. "Did you see it?"

"It was one of those things," said Julie.

She pointed to some golden-colored insects the size of houseflies, buzzing near the trunk of the tree.

"Oh," said Max, "those are wasps."

"Wasps?" said Julie, with rising alarm.

"Yes," said Max, "but this isn't one of the aggressive species. These little guys almost never sting, and when they do, it's very mild. Don't panic."

"Don't panic?" said Julie, with a nervous laugh. "That's easy for you to say." She felt something tickle her arm. She patted her sleeve.

"Are you allergic to the venom of wasps or bees?" said Max, with a note of concern.

"No," said Julie, shaking her head, "I just don't want to get stung, that's all." She again flapped the sides of her shirt. "Where is the darned thing?"

Just then, Julie felt a sharp pricking sensation in the sensitive skin of her underarm. With a cry, she flung off her shirt, stripping down to her tank top, and tossed the shirt to one side.

"Did it sting you?" said Max, stepping forward.

Julie nodded, suddenly unable to speak over the lump of emotion that had formed in her throat. To her dismay, her eyes filled with moisture that spilled over and began running down her cheeks. She bowed her head and watched as her tears splashed onto the platform, creating a pattern of wet marks on the boards.

"Hey, now," said Max, in a soothing manner, "that sting must have really hurt. Come here," he added.

With that, he wrapped his arms around Julie and pulled her close.

Julie twined her arms around Max's waist, giving silent thanks for the presence of his strong, solid frame to lean against at such a vulnerable moment. Pressing her face against his chest, she surrendered herself to an onslaught of feelings. She couldn't have stopped her tears even if she'd wanted to, and her emotions flowed like water escaping from a tap.

"You'll be okay," said Max, his lips murmuring against Julie's brow. He placed a comforting hand at the small of her back. "Everything's going to be all right."

They stood pressed together for a minute or two, entwined in each other's arms and saying nothing. All was still, except for the rustling of leaves, an occasional birdcall, and the sound of Julie quietly sobbing.

Presently, Julie lifted her face from Max's chest and wiped her cheeks.

"Wow," she said, "I didn't see that coming." She gave a shaky laugh. "I guess I needed a good cry, huh?"

"Are you going to be okay?" said Max, maintaining a supportive hold around her waist.

"I think so," said Julie.

"Here," said Max, passing her a clean handkerchief from his pocket.

"Thanks," said Julie. She dried her eyes and returned the handkerchief. "I'm okay now."

Max nodded.

"Sorry to get so worked up," said Julie, feeling embarrassed. "I usually don't fall apart over an insect bite."

She glanced up at Max. His handsome face, a few inches from hers, was tilted toward her as he listened. Julie felt a tingling in the pit of her stomach, as well as a warm sense of safety. Sharing close physical contact with Max was just what she needed at that moment.

"You must think I'm such a wimp," she added.

Max gave a short laugh. "You're not a wimp," he said. "You were startled and you got hurt." He shrugged. "It can happen to anyone."

"Even so," said Julie, brushing some hair from her face, "I can't imagine why I cried like that."

Which wasn't really true. Julie knew why she'd sobbed her heart out. The sting of the wasp had triggered a painful memory. She thought back, recalling with awful clarity the day of Simon's funeral. As she was walking back to her car at the cemetery, following the graveside service, she'd been stung by a bee.

The bee sting had momentarily distracted her from her grief, but she'd later reflected that the wound was like a painful punctuation mark to an already unbearable event. Today on the canopy platform, the sting of the wasp had reminded Julie of the emotional sting of that final parting with Simon.

Julie again glanced up at Max's face, which wore a kindly expression. She considered telling him about Simon's funeral, but then changed her mind. Max was a good listener, but she'd bent his ear enough for one day.

"So, where'd the wasp get you?" said Max, as he and Julie stepped apart.

"Right here," said Julie, showing him a red mark on the inner skin of her upper arm.

"Does it really hurt?" said Max.

"It's not too bad," said Julie. "I've had worse."

"I've got something that'll help," said Max.

He walked over to his backpack and pulled out a first-aid kit. He opened the kit and took out a cotton ball and a little bottle of clear liquid. He uncapped the bottle and moistened the cotton with some of the contents.

"Come and sit here," he said, patting the bench.

Julie sat and then presented her arm.

With gestures that were both competent and gentle, Max cupped Julie's elbow to steady her arm. With his other hand he applied the damp cotton ball to the site of the sting.

"Oh, that feels good," said Julie, focused more on Max's tender ministrations than on the cooling effect of the medication.

"This is an antiseptic," said Max, referring to the lotion. "It'll numb the sting and prevent itching." He regarded Julie. "You must be feeling better," he added. "You're smiling."

"I was just admiring your bedside manner, Doctor Stuart," said Julie, lightly flirting with him.

Just then, Julie remembered how hastily she'd dressed that morning. Unable to locate her bra in the dark, she'd pulled on a tank top without it. Now she was acutely aware that there was nothing covering her breasts but a thin layer of rose-colored silk.

Beneath that wispy layer of silk Julie felt her skin tighten with pleasure as Max applied lotion to her arm. A glance downward confirmed her suspicions. Max's firm but gentle touch was clearly having an effect on her, a natural physical response that was all too apparent.

Julie knew that Max as well had probably noticed the telltale reaction of her body to his touch. But she knew that he'd never let on, so as not to embarrass her. Although Max exuded a potent male presence, he was a true gentleman. Except for the hint of a roguish twinkle in his eye, he was all business as he tended Julie's wound.

"There," he said, closing the first-aid kit, "that ought to do it."

Julie put on her shirt and quickly buttoned it up the front, hiding the physical evidence of Max's effect on her. Feeling warmly flushed and short of breath, she turned away for a moment to compose herself.

When she turned back, she found that Max had shouldered his pack and was glancing at his watch.

"We need to get going," he said. "I have to check some mist nets Ted promised to set up for me early this morning." He looked over at her. "Are you ready?"

"Yep," said Julie, putting on her knapsack and wondering what mist nets were.

"I'll go first," said Max. He grasped the ladder with both hands and stepped backward onto the top rung. "Just follow me and keep close, Julie. Nice and easy now."

They reached the ground a few minutes later. Then, with Max in the lead, they resumed their hike through the forest.

"What's the name of this one?" said Julie, gently untangling a small, brown and gray bird from the mist net.

"Hmm?" said Max, sounding preoccupied. He glanced over at her. "Oh, that's a *Thryothorus genibarbis*," he said, as he measured a finchlike bird he was holding in his hand.

Julie laughed.

"What's so funny?" said Max, releasing the finch and watching it fly into the forest. He jotted something in his notebook.

"You are," said Julie, carefully pulling the fine lines of mesh away from the captured bird's wings. "You keep speaking to me in a foreign language."

"Sorry," said Max, smiling, "force of habit. That lovely specimen you have there is a mustached wren."

"I'll bet it's called that," said Julie, finally freeing the bird and carrying it over to Max, "because of the black-and-white streaking on the side of its face."

"Right you are," said Max, as Julie handed him the wren. He grinned at her. "I'll make a scientist out of you yet."

"Don't count on it," said Julie, teasing him in return. "I've already got a profession, but I will say that this is all very interesting."

For the past couple of hours, Julie had helped Max collect field data for a bird-species census. Working as a team, they'd checked three mist nets that had been stretched across some openings in the forest. Then they had "processed" the live birds that had flown into the nets and been captured.

Made of fine, black threads, the mist nets were practically invisible to any birds flying through the area. Harmlessly ensnared, the birds, after being disentangled from the net, were then weighed, measured, and fitted with numbered leg bands before being released.

Except for pausing to eat some sandwiches and fruit, Max and Julie had worked straight through early afternoon. The mustached wren was their final bird of the day.

"Okay, little guy," said Max, loosening his hold on the wren, "you're free to go."

He held out his hand, palm up, with the wren sitting hunched on it. The wren hesitated for an instant. Then, with an excited chatter and a flick of its tail, it flew away and vanished among the trees.

"We've banded twenty-eight birds," said Max, closing his notebook and tucking it into his backpack. "Not bad for a day's work."

"Was there anything unusual?" said Julie.

"Not really," said Max, as he began dismantling the net and the two lightweight poles supporting it.

"What would happen," said Julie, "if you caught something different?" She helped to collapse the poles into sections, for easier transport.

"You mean," said Max, "a new species?" He added the net and the poles to the other two nets that were already in his backpack.

"Yes," said Julie, "something new."

"Well, if that happened I'd jump up and down and yell with excitement," said Max, with a laugh. He put away his banding kit. "But that's very unlikely. As I told you, the birds in this part of Peru have already been well surveyed and studied."

"But what if you *did* find a new species?" said Julie. "After you jumped up and down, what would you do then?"

"I'd conduct a study," said Max, "and I'd try to get a sense of the bird's population and distribution. I'd set up mist nets, I'd try to get photographs, and I'd take some DNA samples. That sort of thing."

"If you proved that it was a new species," said Julie, "you'd get to name it after yourself, right?"

"Oh, no," said Max, shaking his head. "You never name a newly discovered species after yourself."

"Why not?"

"That would be unprofessional," he said, "and it's just not done. Instead, you name the bird after someone else, someone you admire. It's considered a great honor."

"I see," said Julie.

They worked quietly for a moment, stowing the last of the gear.

"Say," said Max, "didn't I see you sketching earlier?"

"Oh," said Julie, with a shrug, "I was just playing around."

"May I see what you drew?" said Max, taking a seat on a rock.

"Sure," said Julie.

She handed Max her sketching pad. He slowly paged through it.

"Wow, look at this," he said, admiring one of her black-and-white pencil drawings. "Here's the black-capped donacobius we found in the second net." He gave a thoughtful pause. "You have a good eye."

"Thank you," said Julie, pleased by his response.

"The proportions are absolutely correct," said Max, his

eyes on the page, "and all of the details are here. You've even included the light barring on the sides. I can tell at a glance which species it is." He turned his head to regard Julie, who was looking over his shoulder. "Well done."

"I made notes about the colors of its plumage," said Julie, indicating some jottings along the edge of the page.

"Yes, I see that," said Max, nodding.

"I have watercolors back at my cabin," said Julie. "I may do a painting of this bird in my spare time."

"I'd like to see it when you're done," said Max. He turned the page. "Oh, here's one of the Amazonian royal flycatchers we banded." He paused. "Look at that. It's all there. You've included the crest, the barring on the chest, and even the rictal bristles."

"The what?" said Julie.

"Rictal bristles," repeated Max. He pointed to the head. "That's what these hairlike filaments around the beak are called."

"Oh, I see."

Max continued to study the drawing in silence. Then he said, "I, uh, have a confession to make."

"A confession?" said Julie. "What do you mean?"

"I feel a little sheepish," said Max. "When you showed me your drawing of the orchid, I thought it was good."

"And you told me so," said Julie, remembering.

"Yes," said Max, "but what I also thought at the time was that it might only be a coincidence that your drawing had turned out as well as it did." He stared at the picture of the flycatcher. "I obviously misjudged your level of talent. You are consistently good at this, Julie."

"Why, thank you," said Julie. "That's nice of you to say."

"You certainly have more artistic ability," said Max, "than any business major I've ever met before."

"I've always loved art," said Julie. "I took a few classes in college, but I've mostly taught myself."

"These are incredibly accurate," said Max, indicating her drawings. "You would have made an excellent illustrator."

"Maybe it's not too late," said Julie, pondering the possibilities. "My life is at a crossroads," she added. "Maybe art will play more of a role in my future."

"I definitely think it should," said Max, as he began turning the page to the next drawing.

"Oh no!" cried Julie, suddenly remembering something. "Don't look at that one."

"Now don't be shy," said Max. "I want to see what other species you've drawn."

Julie reached for her sketching pad, but she was too late. Max had already turned to the next drawing. She stood in mortified silence as he stared long and hard at the page. Then he chuckled under his breath.

"Well, well," he said, his deep voice laced with both pleasure and amusement, "what have we here?" He shot a teasing glance in Julie's direction. "Birds were apparently not the only thing on your mind today."

"You weren't meant to see that," said Julie, almost choking on her embarrassment. She felt her face and neck flush with warmth.

"It's a good likeness," said Max, with a roguish twinkle in his eye.

"Please give it to me," said Julie.

"But I want to admire it," said Max. "It isn't every day that I have my portrait drawn."

Julie cringed, wishing with all her heart that the earth would open up and swallow her.

But Max was obviously feeling anything but uncomfortable. In fact, Julie could tell that he was thoroughly enjoying himself.

Max held up the sketching pad for a closer appraisal. He turned Julie's full-page drawing of him this way and that, as if pretending to be an art critic.

"Yes, indeed," he said, "this is a good likeness. But," he

added, as a devilish smile crossed his face, "haven't you left something out?"

Julie groaned, her cheeks on fire.

"This must be what they call artistic license," continued Max, with a gust of laughter. He pointed to the drawing. "Is that what this is, Julie? Because I seem to be naked from the waist up."

Chapter Seven

I must have a little touch of amnesia," said Max, chuckling. He remained seated on the rock while gazing at Julie's full-page drawing of him.

"What do you mean?" said Julie.

"Well, I have absolutely no memory," said Max, "of posing for you with my shirt off." He arched a brow in her direction. "But I'd be happy to anytime."

"Okay, you've had your fun," said Julie, assuming a tone of righteous indignation.

Julie knew that she wasn't doing a very good job of concealing how awkward she felt. It didn't matter what she said. She could feel that her burning cheeks were giving her away.

"You weren't meant to see that," she went on, feeling like a fool. "Now please give it to me."

Max rose to his feet and handed Julie her sketching pad.

Julie hastily closed the cover and thrust the pad into her knapsack. She'd never been so embarrassed in her life.

That'll teach me to make surreptitious drawings, she silently scolded herself, as she cinched the drawstring on her knapsack.

"I do have a few suggestions for that portrait of me," said Max, with a twinkle in his eye.

"May we please just drop the subject?" said Julie. "Can't you see how embarrassed I am? I had no intention for you to see that."

"But it's a good drawing," said Max. "It shows off your, um, lively imagination," he added. "How else would you be able to draw me with my shirt off?"

"I told you," said Julie, still flustered, "that I was just playing around with my sketching today."

"Clearly," said Max, with understated amusement.

"I took a figure-study class in college," said Julie, trying to explain. "While you were working today, I wondered if I could make a drawing of your, um, upper physique, based only on what I could tell from the way your, um, upper arms, that is your biceps, moved, and, um, how your shoulders pressed against the cloth of your shirt, and the way the muscles in your back flexed whenever you—"

She halted, aware that she was babbling. Her nervous avalanche of words was making things worse, not better.

"Go on," said Max, crossing his arms over his chest. "Don't stop now. I find this all very interesting."

"My sketching you," said Julie, lifting her chin, "was an art challenge."

"An art challenge," repeated Max, amusement tugging at the corners of his mouth.

"That's right," said Julie, maintaining her dignity. Then she added, "I'm sorry if you feel spied upon. I had no intention of invading your privacy by neglecting to include your shirt in my figure study."

"Oh, I'm not the least bit offended," said Max, slanting a smile at her. "In fact, I find it rather flattering to have someone think of me as a subject worthy of a—what did you call it?—a figure study." He tilted his head at her. "You may spy on me whenever you like."

"Oh, I think I'll probably stick to drawing birds from now on," said Julie, with a self-conscious laugh. She touched her flaming cheek, wishing again that the earth would swallow her up.

Having Max accidentally see the drawing was bad enough. But knowing that he might be speculating about Julie's reasons for portraying him partially disrobed was even worse. Everything Julie had said was true. She'd honestly wondered if she could compose a figure study based solely on what she could perceive beneath Max's shirt.

But not even Julie had known, until that very moment, that there was more to her drawing exercise than artistic curiosity. She was having romantic fantasies about Max. Drawing him naked from the waist up advertised that fact, loud and clear.

"Don't be embarrassed," said Max. "Besides," he added, with a throaty chuckle, "it could've been worse. You could've drawn me wearing nothing from head to toe but my birthday suit. Now *that* would've been awkward."

Julie groaned.

"But, back to my suggestions," said Max, stroking his chin in the way of an art professor launching into a critique.

To Julie's chagrin, Max was clearly determined to extract every last atom of fun from the incident. She braced herself for some spoofing, knowing that she probably had it coming.

"For one thing," said Max, "I have a bit more hair on my chest than what you drew."

Julie caught her breath at this intimate revelation.

"And," he continued, "you left out my tattoo."

"You have a tattoo?" said Julie, voicing curiosity despite herself.

"Yep," said Max, nodding, "it's a great, big stars-and-stripes banner that says 'Mom and apple pie.' It goes clear across my chest, from one side to the other. It moves whenever I flex my pectoral muscles." He gave her a wolfish grin and made as if to unbutton his shirt. "Care to see it?"

"Okay, enough with the teasing," said Julie, pretending to scold him. "You've had enough fun for one day."

Max laughed.

"Now what's our next job?" said Julie, changing the subject. She put on her knapsack.

"It involves photography," said Max, strapping on his back-pack. "If we're lucky, we'll get some pictures of a gorgeous female named Trixie."

"Who's Trixie?" asked Julie, falling in behind Max as he headed down the trail. "Is she another tarantula, like Lucy?"

"You'll see," said Max, glancing over his shoulder. "No hints until we get there. Oh, and feel free to sketch me as we walk," he added, chuckling one last time.

Julie rolled her eyes at him.

"Can you spot the electronic sensor?" asked Max, speaking to Julie in a quiet voice.

It was half an hour later. Max and Julie were standing near a photographic device mounted on a tree, about three feet off the ground.

Julie looked around.

"Is that the sensor?" she asked, pointing to a metal object the size of a bicycle reflector. The object was mounted on a tree opposite the camera.

"That's it," said Max, nodding. "This setup is called a camera trap. Whenever an animal passes between the sensor and the camera, the camera takes a picture. It even works at night, with the help of a harmless infrared flash."

"Do you ever get photos of jaguars?" asked Julie, picturing those regal jungle cats in her mind.

"Sometimes," said Max, opening a hatch on the metal housing that protected the camera from the elements. "We get pictures of all kinds of critters. Monkeys, giant anteaters, you name it. It just depends on what's passing through the area. We never know what we're going to get."

"Hmm," said Julie, watching him work.

Max withdrew a photo cartridge from the camera and dropped it into his pack.

"We'll look at that tonight," he said. "Maybe it'll have a picture of Trixie on it."

"And who, exactly, is Trixie?" said Julie, as Max reloaded the camera with a fresh cartridge.

"Trixie's a tapir," said Max, closing the hatch.

"What's a tapir?" asked Julie. She'd never heard the word before.

"It's a big, gentle vegetarian mammal," said Max. "Tapirs are about the size of a small cow. In fact, they're sometimes called jungle cows."

"I see."

"Tapirs are shy and nocturnal," said Max. "That's why we have to resort to trickery, such as this camera trap, to monitor their behavior."

"I'd like to see a tapir," said Julie, already planning to sketch the animal with the curious-sounding name.

"Your best chance for that," said Max, hoisting his backpack, "is at the tapir salt lick."

"What's that?" said Julie.

"It's a muddy pond about a thirty-minute walk from camp," said Max, buckling his waist strap. "Trixie and her pals go to the pond every night to wallow and eat minerals from the soil. I'll take you to the viewing platform some night, if you're interested."

"Oh, I am."

"We may have to spend the night there," said Max. "It all depends on when the tapirs decide to show up." He regarded Julie. "Would that be okay with you? Spending the night, I mean."

"Uh, sure," said Julie, trying to sound casual, even though her heart had just done a somersault at the idea of spending a night with Max. "I was a Girl Scout, remember. I don't mind camping out as long as I have someone with me."

"All right, then," said Max. "We'll do that." He checked his watch. "It'll be dark soon. Let's start heading back."

"There she is," said Max, studying an image on his computer screen. "That's a good picture of Trixie."

"What an interesting-looking animal," said Julie, seated beside Max. They were reviewing the pictures on the photo cartridge they'd collected from the forest that day. "Hmm, long nose, short legs, and with a body a bit like a cow's." She turned to Max. "But how do you know for sure that this is Trixie and not some other tapir?"

"Because she's the only tapir around here," said Max, "with a dark patch above her left eye." He touched the screen. "It's right there."

"Oh, I see," said Julie, nodding.

It was after dinner. Max and Julie were sitting in Max's combination living area and study, located on the upper level of a two-story building behind the dining hall. The room had the spacious feeling of a loft, with exposed rafters and a high-pitched ceiling lined with thatch.

Julie glanced around at the interesting scientific clutter. Bookshelves and file cabinets lined the walls, and photographs of birds hung from the rafters. Notebooks and scientific journals spilled onto the floor. The surface of Max's desk held an array of rain forest artifacts: river stones, labeled jars of soil samples, leaves drying in a plant press, a tiny bird's nest, a blue feather with an identification tag.

Julie took a relaxed breath, feeling at ease amid the intimate and telling objects with which Max had surrounded himself. His private sanctuary was like a mini natural history museum, with masculine touches here and there. A shirt carelessly flung over the back of a canvas chair. An open shaving kit spied through a doorway into the bathroom. A well-worn pair of moccasins tossed under the rumpled bed.

"Care for some wine?" said Max, breaking the silence.

"I'd love some," said Julie.

Max rose from his chair, rummaged in the bottom drawer of a file cabinet, and came up with a bottle of red wine and two glasses. He cleared a space on his desk for the two glasses, and then he poured the wine and handed one of the glasses to Julie.

"Cheers," he said, raising his glass.

"Cheers," said Julie, and they each took a sip.

They continued reviewing the photos for a few minutes, exclaiming over pictures of other tapirs and a herd of rain forest pigs. Max called out the name of each species as its image appeared on the screen. Many of the creatures Julie had never heard of before.

As the rich burgundy wine warmed Julie's throat, she felt a deep sense of contentment. The darkness of the rain forest pressed against the screened windows with the intimate comfort of black velvet. A branch bearing yellow flowers rustled against one of the screens, releasing a spicy fragrance, and the songs of frogs and crickets throbbed in the air.

Stealing a glance at Max's strong profile, Julie realized that there was nowhere else she'd rather be. Max's private lair was the perfect retreat. It was like an eagle's aerie high above the earth, and it was a pleasure to be there with him.

"Well, that's it," said Max, as they came to the last picture. He turned off the screen. "We got about a dozen species that time."

He jotted something in a notebook and then tossed the notebook onto a pile.

"It's been a long day," he said, rubbing the back of his neck. He regarded Julie. "You held up pretty well, I must say."

"Of course," said Julie, with a touch of pride. "What did you expect?"

"Oh, that I'd walk your socks off," said Max, with wry amusement. He swallowed some wine. "You insisted on shadowing me, so I'd planned on wearing you out. That way you'd never want to tag along with me again."

"Ouch," said Julie, pretending to wince, "that doesn't sound very friendly."

"Truth is," said Max, with a touch of chagrin, "I was feeling anything but friendly toward you on that certain point. I mean, why would I want someone right on my heels all day? But, um—"

He paused, his demeanor that of a man waging an inner debate. How much did he want to reveal?

"Yes?" asked Julie, coaxing him to continue. She twirled her glass, admiring how the wine reflected the light.

"But, once again," said Max, running a hand over the square plane of his jaw, "you've surprised me."

"How so?" said Julie, tracing the stem of her glass with her thumb and forefinger.

"As I've said, credit where it's due," said Max. "Not only did you keep up, but you were useful out there. You never once got in my way, and, best of all, you seemed genuinely interested in everything we did."

"I *am* interested," said Julie, and she meant it.

"I can't believe I'm saying this," said Max, with a brief shake of his head, "but I'm actually glad you came along today." He leaned toward Julie and clinked his glass against hers. "So here's to good help and to, um, good company."

"I'll drink to that," said Julie, feeling a warm, satisfied glow as she raised her glass to her lips.

They sat in reflective silence for a moment or two. Then Julie spoke.

"I was determined to keep up with you today," she said. "But I had the easy part, if you think about it."

"What do you mean?" said Max.

"All I had to carry was my little knapsack," said Julie, "but you had that enormous pack on your back. It looked like it weighed about forty pounds."

"I don't have to carry that much every day," said Max, "but

sometimes it's unavoidable." He slowly rolled his head from side to side. "My muscles are sore tonight, no doubt about it."

"Maybe I can help," said Julie, acting on impulse.

Setting her glass aside, Julie rose from her seat and stood behind Max's chair. Laying her hands on him, she began massaging his tight muscles, kneading her way along his shoulders and upper arms.

"How's that?" she asked, feeling the warmth from Max's body spreading through her fingers and palms.

"Are you kidding?" said Max, with a little groan. "It's incredible." He closed his eyes, submitting to Julie's touch with the languid pleasure of a big cat. "This is just what I needed."

There followed several minutes of silence, broken only by the muted sounds of the forest and Max's relaxed breathing. As Julie worked with her fingers, feeling for tightness and manipulating the soreness from Max's shoulders, she felt a deep connection with both the present moment and with the man himself. She reflected on the mystery of the human touch, a powerful force that could both calm and stimulate at the same time.

Max broke the silence.

"I've been thinking about those figures you showed to me today," he said. "You know, the ones from Pierson-Roth."

As her hands continued massaging, Julie could hear warning bells going off in her head at the mention of the Pierson-Roth Foundation. She disliked having conflict intrude on the moment, but she supposed there was no avoiding it.

"What about the figures?" she said, and braced herself for another debate.

"Those numbers are hard to argue with," said Max, tipping his head forward as Julie rubbed his neck. "Things are worse than I realized."

"Yes, money's tight right now," said Julie, glad to hear that Max might be starting to face reality.

"You know that I've never liked the idea of tourists coming to Manu River," said Max.

"You've made that very clear," said Julie, kneading with her thumbs.

"I'm still not wild about the plan," said Max, "but I've thought of a compromise I think I can live with."

"A compromise?" said Julie.

She was finding it hard to focus on Max's words while her hands were in such intimate contact with the warm, bare skin of his neck. She tried to keep her mind on business, and yet she found herself longing to run her fingers through Max's hair or to lean against him and rest her cheek on his shoulder.

"What do you have in mind?" she said.

"Day trips," said Max.

"What do you mean?" said Julie, not understanding.

"I'm talking about ecotourists visiting Manu River," said Max, "on a day-trip basis. They'd pay a fee to come here and have a look around, but they wouldn't spend the night. They'd sleep somewhere else."

"Where?"

"At Laguna Miguel."

"You mean, the village downriver from here?"

"That's right."

"But that's an hour-long boat ride each way," said Julie, hardly believing her ears. "You'd expect people to make a two-hour round-trip on the river in order to visit the research station?"

"Sure, why not?" said Max, giving a little shrug. "You said yourself that this area is unique, and it is. I'm sure people would pay to take day trips here."

"But think of how inconvenient that would be."

"How so?"

"I believe that most people," said Julie, talking while she massaged, "would want to come here and settle in for a two- or three-day stay. For many of them, it would be their one and only trip to the rain forest, and they'd want to get a genuine feeling for the place. I know I would. You can't ask people to spend hours every day ferrying up and down the river."

"But they'd love it," said Max, insisting on his point of view. "There's plenty to see out on the water and along the shore."

"And another thing," said Julie, running a list of objections through her mind. "Does Laguna Miguel have tourist facilities?"

"Not yet," said Max, "but that's easy to fix. The village can build some cabins and an outdoor dining area. It's a good plan, Julie."

"Hmm, I don't know," she said, sounding doubtful.

"Besides," said Max, "it's a good way to help the village. Laguna Miguel has a tiny school, but they need books. And they're always short on medical supplies. By sharing the tourist dollars, both Manu River and the village would benefit." He paused. "Don't you see? It's perfect."

Julie said nothing for a moment. She continued massaging Max's neck and shoulders as she silently weighed the pros and cons of his suggestion.

On the one hand, he wanted to help the village, which was a worthy motive. As the director of the research station, he'd already boosted Laguna Miguel's economy by hiring carpenters and other staff who earned a good wage at Manu River. Now he saw a way to do even more for the village and Julie didn't doubt his sincerity for a moment.

On the other hand, Max wasn't exactly making it easy for ecotourists to visit the research station. Under his plan, they'd come, they'd have a quick look, and then, just as they were beginning to get a sense of the place, they'd have to turn around and leave.

The logistics of having visitors sleep elsewhere were both cumbersome and counterproductive. Julie could imagine people grumbling about having to endure another long river trip at the end of the day.

And who could blame them? It would be so much better to

stay right where they were. That way they could sample Hernando's excellent cooking, take part in stimulating dinner conversation with students and scientists, and watch night fall at Manu River. In Julie's opinion, that would be the ideal ecotourism experience.

By being required to return to the village in the afternoon, however, visitors would miss some of the most magical experiences Manu River had to offer. No matter how accommodating the village was, Julie knew that spending the night there could not compare with sleeping in the peaceful embrace of the rain forest.

Julie was grateful that Max finally seemed ready to work with her. She counted that as progress. But was his idea feasible? And, more importantly, would Pierson-Roth go for the plan?

Max's voice broke in on Julie's inner dialogue.

"You're being awfully quiet," he said. "I guess my idea has caught you by surprise."

"Yes, it has," admitted Julie, "but I'll certainly give it full consideration."

"I think it's the perfect solution," said Max, sounding as if it were already a done deal.

"Well, I'm not ready to concede that," said Julie, with a short laugh. "Your heart's in the right place, Max. It's wonderful to want to help the village, but—" She hesitated.

"But what?"

"I'm concerned about the logistics," said Julie. "It would be so inconvenient to have to ferry people back and forth on the river. It would waste both time and fuel."

"Okay," said Max, "what else?"

"People will want to stay here, Max," said Julie. "This is a real, honest-to-goodness research facility, and it presents a unique experience for visitors. Once people see Manu River, they'll want to spend several days and nights here, just soaking it all up.

"I'm also wondering," she went on, "about cost-effectiveness.

With your plan, would the research station earn enough money to stay open? You'd be sharing the revenue with the village—which is not a bad thing, mind you—but would you be left with enough income to stay afloat?" She paused. "I hate to sound preachy, but you have to think about your bottom line."

"I know," said Max, "but you'll factor all of this into your report, won't you?"

"Of course," said Julie, "and I'll be happy to recommend your plan to the board if the figures support it. Give me a couple of days to crunch some numbers, and I'll get back to you."

"Fair enough," said Max, putting the topic to rest. "Now, just keep doing what you're doing," he said, arching his neck with pleasure. "I could get used to this."

Several minutes went by as Julie continued to knead the soreness from Max's back muscles. The scents and the sounds of the night forest wafted through the open windows. A gecko chirped, and a large, colorful moth with trailing wings fluttered against the outer surface of one of the screens. All seemed right with the world.

Julie felt a deep sense of peace as her fingers worked their magic. She'd missed having a man to tenderly fuss over, and she yearned for someone to once again share life's experiences with. Being on her own for the past year had taught her resilience and self-reliance, and she was grateful for those lessons. Now, however, she was ready to open her heart to someone else. Was Max the one?

As if somehow reading her thoughts, Max reached for Julie's wrist. Then, as if it were the most natural thing in the world, he drew Julie's hand to his face, pressed her palm against his cheek, and held it there.

Several potent moments of silent communication ticked by. Julie blinked away a quick stab of tears, her heart instantly recognizing what Max was telling her. With this simple, intimate gesture—pressing her palm to his cheek—he was conveying that he, too, longed for companionship. He too yearned for a soul mate.

Julie had wondered if Max had become wary of relationships, following his wife's betrayal and the breakup of his marriage. If that was the case, who could blame him? But she knew that even Max—strong, capable, self-sufficient man that he was—couldn't bury himself in his work and turn his back on love forever.

Yes, even Max needed a soft place to fall. By pressing Julie's hand to his cheek, he was responding to the human heart's oldest equation on earth: One man, one woman, mutual attraction, and a shared yearning not to be alone anymore.

"Oh, Max," murmured Julie, her voice catching as she bent forward and leaned against him. Twining her other arm around his neck, she rested her cheek against his hair.

"Julie," whispered Max, and kissed her wrist.

Then he rose from his chair, turned around to face Julie, and gathered her in his arms. With an expression of great tenderness, he tipped her face toward his and lowered his lips for a kiss.

Before their lips could meet, however, Max and Julie were interrupted by the sound of knocking at the door.

"Doctor Max," called a male voice, from out on the landing, "are you in there?"

"What perfect timing," growled Max, as he and Julie stepped apart. "Yes," he called, raising his voice, "who is it?"

"It's Ted."

"Come on in," said Max, running a hand through his hair. "What can I do for you, Moth Man?" he said, as Ted entered the room.

"Oh, hi, Julie," said Ted, noticing her standing by Max's desk. He turned back to Max. "The kitchen generator's acting up. Hernando can't seem to fix it, so he sent me to get you."

"Hmm," said Max, with a little frown. "I hope it's nothing serious. I'd better go and see what the problem is."

He turned to Julie, communicating with his eyes. "I, um, shouldn't be long," he said. He handed her a file folder from his desk. "Here's the information on morpho butterflies I was telling you about."

"Oh, thanks," said Julie, her heart still pounding from their intimate encounter. "I'll take a look."

"Right, okay," said Max, his body language telling Julie that the last thing he wanted to do was to leave her company. "I'll see you later, then," he added, as he followed Ted toward the door.

Julie gave a little wave and watched the door close behind Max and Ted. She heard their footfalls on the steps outside and then all was silent. Taking a deep breath, she waged a brief inner debate. Should she stay and await Max's return, or should she go?

Julie decided to stay.

She poured herself another half-glass of wine and then settled into a comfortable chair. Stifling a yawn—it had been a long day, after all—she opened the folder on morpho butterflies and began to read.

Julie awoke a few hours later. She was lying on a bed, fully clothed except for her shoes. A soft blanket covered her and her head was resting on a pillow. She'd been having the most wonderful dream, but now its wispy images faded as she gazed up at a thatched ceiling and wondered where she was.

She raised herself on one elbow and looked around, trying to get her bearings. A lantern burned low in one corner, bathing the room in an amber glow. Seeing the bird photographs and the walls of books, Julie realized that she was still in Max's study.

Max himself was reclining in a slung-back chair. His fingers were laced together in his lap, and his long legs were stretched out in front of him. He was sound asleep.

Julie rubbed her eyes and glanced at a bedside clock. It was three o'clock in the morning. She tossed off the blanket, slid her legs over the side of the bed, and put on her shoes. Moving quietly, she took the blanket from the bed and then tiptoed over to Max's slumbering form and tucked it around him.

She stood there for a moment, her heart expanding with tenderness and longing. Max's head rested to one side, in the heroic attitude of a piece of classical sculpture. His cheeks and his jaw line were relaxed, his skin faintly shadowed with beard stubble. His chest rose and fell as he gently breathed in and out.

Julie's eyes lingered on the sensual curve of Max's lips, and on the lock of dark hair that had tumbled across his brow. He reminded her of a warrior in repose. He'd wanted to kiss her the night before, and would have had it not been for Ted's untimely arrival.

As she gazed down at Max, Julie had to fight the sweet impulse to lean forward and awaken him with a kiss. Instead, she let him sleep.

Julie knew what must have happened after Max and Ted left the study. The physical exertions of her long day out in the field, combined with the relaxing effects of the wine, had lulled her senses. She didn't remember dozing off, but she'd obviously done so.

Later, when Max returned to his study, he'd found Julie asleep in the chair. Julie had only the haziest recollection of being lifted by a pair of strong arms and deposited on a comfortable surface. Max had removed her shoes and covered her with a blanket. Then he'd taken the chair for himself.

Julie silently thanked Max for his thoughtfulness. Then she tiptoed from the room, quietly closing the door behind her.

Chapter Eight

Okay, everybody grab something," said Max, indicating a pile of boxes and canvas bags on the ground near the dining hall. "Let's get this stuff down to the boat in one trip."

It was after breakfast the next morning. Max and Julie were helping Fran and Robert move their filming equipment and camping gear to a site upriver. The two students had located another family of giant river otters living in a peaceful backwater, or oxbow. Their plan was to camp on the oxbow for several days to film the otters.

It would take an hour to travel upriver by boat, and another half hour to transport the gear overland to the oxbow. Once Max and Julie had helped Fran and Robert set up their camp, they would take their leave and return to the research station.

"All right," said Max, "here we go."

He shouldered one of the backpacks and tucked a duffel bag under each arm. Then, with Julie and the others falling in behind him with the rest of the gear, Max started down the trail leading to the boat dock.

116

Once they reached the dock, they loaded the gear into a long, motorized boat with a canvas awning. Soon they were under way, with Max at the tiller. Julie was sitting beside Max, and Fran and Robert were sitting together in the bow, facing forward.

It was a beautiful, sunny day, with a cooling breeze wafting off the river. The edges of the awning flapped in the wind, and water splashed against the sides of the boat.

Julie gazed around at the passing scenery. Dense rain forest hugged the shores. The course of the Manu River twisted this way and that, exposing sandbars, muddy banks, and tiny islands with sparse vegetation.

A pair of scarlet macaws flew overhead, their loud, raucous calls audible over the purring of the motor. Julie pointed out the birds to Max. He nodded, and swung the boat around a floating log.

The morning had been filled with activity and busy preparations for the boat trip. Julie and Max had exchanged long glances during the communal breakfast, but there hadn't been an opportunity for any private conversation.

All they could do was smile across the table at each other as if they shared a secret, which they did. The memory of their embrace the night before, and of the kiss that hadn't quite happened—but which surely would in the future—seemed to sizzle in the air between them like a hot flame, as tempting as honey. Julie barely tasted her eggs and toast, because her mind was so distracted by thoughts of what it would be like to kiss Max.

Now, as Max steered the boat through a straight stretch, he leaned toward Julie and spoke privately in her ear.

"Thanks for putting that blanket over me last night," he said.

"I was just returning the favor," said Julie, smiling at him. "Besides, I should be thanking you. After all, you gave up your bed."

"Oh, I was glad to do it," said Max. His tone told Julie that sleeping in the same room with her more than made up for any discomfort he'd had to endure.

Julie gazed at the light glancing off the water and mused to herself. She'd awakened in her cabin that morning with a mix of emotions, and now she had a lot to think over.

Regarding the conflict that centered on Pierson-Roth's plan for the Manu River facility, Julie was grateful that Max had made some concessions. He now recognized the seriousness of the Foundation's financial situation, and his attitude had evolved from stubborn intractability to one of cooperation. He'd even come up with a compromise.

But would Max's plan remedy the research station's financial shortfall? That remained to be seen.

On a personal level, Julie sensed that her relationship with Max had turned a corner as well. Her initial attraction to him, that of a woman drawn to a strong alpha male, was now balanced by emotions that ran deep and true.

Max was the sexiest man Julie had ever met. Her fantasies of being held in his arms and kissing him brought a flush to her cheeks and a tingling in her stomach.

But she knew that there was more than animal magnetism at work. As she got to know Max, she recognized his strong sense of character and his kindness. His joyful, giving personality, as well as his passion for his work, had stirred Julie's imagination and made her heart sing with possibilities.

She stole a glance at Max's profile, his watchful gaze forward and his hair ruffled by the wind. Her heart squeezed with longing. Although she barely knew Max, Julie sensed how easy it would be to fall for him.

"Look," said Max, interrupting Julie's thoughts. He was pointing toward some dark, furry shapes lounging in a tree near the shore. "Howler monkeys," he said.

Julie nodded.

"See what I mean?" said Max, shooting Julie an I-told-you-so look. "There's a lot to observe along the river."

Julie nodded again, knowing that Max was making a case for his plan. He wanted tourists visiting Manu River to sleep in Laguna Miguel instead of at the research station.

She leaned toward him, brushing against his shoulder.

"I know what you're up to," she said, lightly teasing him. "You say you want to help the village, and I believe you. Really, I do. But you've got a personal agenda as well."

"What do you mean?" said Max, guiding the boat around a sandbar.

"I'm sure," said Julie, "that you wouldn't at all mind seeing the last of the tourists at the end of the day. In fact, you'd welcome that." She laughed. "I can almost picture you down at the dock, waving good-bye as the 'intruders' disappear downriver and leave you in peace."

"Ah, you read me like a book," said Max, keeping his eyes forward, the corners of his mouth twitching. Julie could tell that her words had hit home.

"Well, Max," she said, "you may have to adjust both your attitude and your agenda. If the numbers I'm working on don't support your plan, you'll just have to get used to having visitors underfoot a bit more than you'd like. Forcing them to sleep in the village is not a workable idea, in my opinion."

"I am *not* going to baby-sit a bunch of tourists," said Max, frowning. "If you have your way, you'll turn the research station into a kind of Amazonian Club Med."

"Don't be silly," said Julie, getting her dander up. "First of all, you'd hire a manager to deal with the tourism end of things. Which means you'd have little if anything to do with visitors, if that's what you wanted. You could continue your work uninterrupted."

Max said nothing.

"For that matter," she added, "you could hide out in the forest all day and eat dinner in your room. That way, you'd avoid all contact with them."

"That's ridiculous," said Max, skewering her with a steely look. "I'm not antisocial, for Pete's sake. I'm simply trying to protect the scientific integrity of the research station, something you nonscientists wouldn't understand. Having visitors leave at the end of the day is a good idea." He faced forward. "I've come up with a very workable compromise."

"And that's your best offer, right?" said Julie, with a touch of sarcasm. "Well, I'm sorry," she added, "but the final decision is not up to you. The board at Pierson-Roth holds the purse strings, and they will decide how best to keep Manu River's financial affairs in the black." She paused before delivering the final thrust. "With or without you."

Max gave an impatient sigh and stared ahead, his brows lowered like storm clouds. Julie could imagine smoke billowing from his ears—he seemed that angry.

Max and Julie spent the rest of the boat ride in stony silence. They sat away from each other, avoiding physical contact, their eyes on the water.

Julie felt a pang of longing whenever she glanced at Fran and Robert, seated in the bow. In contrast with Julie and the fuming Max, Fran and Robert were sitting nestled as close to each other as they could get.

Robert had wrapped an affectionate arm around Fran, and now and then Fran offered her lips for a little kiss. In the manner of doting lovers everywhere, Fran and Robert had spun a magical cocoon around themselves and were living in a sweet, little world all their own. Population: two.

For Julie, the journey upriver seemed to last forever, due to the chilly atmosphere between her and Max. She sighed with relief when Max finally cut the engine and allowed the bow of the boat to slide up onto a sandbar. Robert jumped out with a rope, pulled the boat farther onto the shore, and then tied the rope to a tree trunk.

"Well," said Max, speaking quietly so that only Julie could hear him, "you and I managed to ruin the boat ride for each other. Are we going to do the same on the hike to the oxbow?" He looked at her. "Or shall we call a truce?"

"I'll vote for a truce if you will," said Julie. She tried to smile, even though her feelings were still in turmoil over some of Max's earlier argumentative comments.

"All right," said Max, with a little nod, "truce it is." He raised his voice. "Okay, everyone, let's unload this stuff and start moving it to the oxbow."

"Oh, look," breathed Julie, "there's one of the otters now."

"It's the older of the two females," whispered Fran, who was standing beside Julie. "She has a baby with her. Do you see it?"

"Yes, now I do," said Julie, entranced by the sinewy creatures swimming in the still water. Each of the two graceful bodies left a wide, rippling V in its wake.

Julie, Max, and the others had carried the supplies and camping gear to a flat, sandy spot overlooking the oxbow. They'd pitched the tent and rain tarp, set up the propane cooking stove, and unpacked the filming equipment. Now the four of them were assembled on the bank of the oxbow, admiring the giant otter and her baby.

"How many otters live here, you figure?" asked Max, watching the swimmers through a pair of binoculars.

"At least six," said Robert, photographing the female and her baby as he talked. "Maybe more."

"They're beautiful," said Julie, commenting on the otters' rich pelts of cream and chocolate brown. "And they have such long, spiky whiskers."

"I love their eyes," said Fran. "They're so big and expressive." She jotted something in a notebook. "When they look right at you, you'd swear they were as intelligent as you or me."

"Oh, they're very intelligent," said Robert.

"And they're so at home in the water," said Max, following the otters' movements. "They're as graceful as dolphins."

"I envy you being able to camp here for a few days," said Julie, speaking to Fran and Robert. "This is a gorgeous area. You're going to get some wonderful footage."

They all stood there for a few more minutes, admiring the otters. They laughed softly when the little one playfully nudged its mother and then captured a floating stick in its mouth and shook it like a rambunctious puppy.

Presently, Max checked the time and looked over at Julie.

"We'd better get back to the boat," he said. He turned to Fran and Robert. "You two all set here? You've got the satellite-phone, in case you need to call the station."

"We're fine," they said.

"All right, then," said Max, taking a final look around. "Someone will come and get you in three days." He clapped Robert on the shoulder. "Be safe, you two."

It took Max and Julie about thirty minutes to retrace their steps through the forest. When they arrived at the river, they paused at the top of the sloping bank leading down to the boat.

"Looks like we might get some rain," said Max, glancing skyward.

"A big storm or a shower?" asked Julie, thinking about Fran and Robert back at their camp.

"I'd say shower," said Max. "It shouldn't last long."

Julie and Max walked down the slope, reaching the boat just as the clouds opened up and sent forth a drenching rain. They sat under the protective awning, sheltered from the downpour. The rain pounded on the canvas and ran off the edges in rivulets. Droplets dimpled the river and a fresh breeze rattled the palms growing along the bank.

They'd left the boat tied to the shore, having decided to wait for the rain to subside before casting off. Julie stowed her knapsack and then removed her boots and socks to be more comfortable on the ride downriver.

Max followed suit. Then the two of them watched the rain together, like two barefooted kids having a grand adventure.

Soon the rain let up and the sun came out. The light sparkled on the water, and steamy condensation rose from the trees. Birds that had been silent during the brief downpour began singing again. Somewhere in the distance, a howler monkey roared out his dominance as the alpha male in his tribe.

"Uh-oh," said Julie, suddenly remembering something.

"What is it?" said Max. He'd stepped from the boat, but had not yet untied the line.

"I accidentally left my plant samples up there," said Julie, pointing to the bank above the river. She was referring to the bouquet of leaves and flowers she'd collected on their hike back to the river. "I want to sketch those."

"Want me to get them?" said Max.

"No, that's okay," said Julie. "I'll do it."

She swung her legs over the side of the boat and crossed the sandbar. The sand was warm and damp, the texture of the fine grains working like a massage on the bottoms of her bare feet. It felt wonderful to be free of her confining boots for a change.

When Julie reached the gentle slope beyond the sand, she found that the rain had turned the dirt to mud. She took a couple of steps, enjoying how the slippery mud, which felt like liquidized satin, molded to the shape of her heels and squished between her toes.

Julie hadn't walked barefoot in mud since she was a child, wading on a riverbank in the Pacific Northwest. But that chilly activity was nothing compared to the sensual experience of having the warm, oozy, tropical mud of the Manu River caress her naked feet.

"Hey, this is fun," she called back to Max.

Then she cried out as she lost her balance and her feet slipped from under her. Down she tumbled, landing on her bottom in the soft mud. She started laughing as Max ran to help her.

"Are you okay?" he asked, extending his hand.

"Oh, I'm very okay," she said, gripping his palm. "I'm just being a kid again." She gave him a mischievous smile. "Won't you join me?"

Acting on impulse, Julie tugged on Max's hand, sending him sprawling beside her. Max yelped, caught off guard. With another laugh, Julie reached over and daubed mud on his cheek.

"Okay, woman," said Max, growling in play, "you asked for it."

Running his finger through the mud, Max painted a stripe across Julie's forehead and another one down the length of her neck.

Julie squealed with fun and then giggled as Max's muddy finger traced the sensitive hollow at the base of her throat. Pretending to want to escape, she gave Max a little push and rolled to one side. She grabbed a fistful of mud and tossed it at his chest. It connected with a plop and slid down his shirt, leaving a muddy track in its wake.

"Hey," he said, roaring in mock outrage, "this is a clean shirt."

"Not anymore," said Julie, and made an impish face at him.

"Okay, if that's how you want it," said Max, his eyes smoldering with a bad-boy twinkle, "then it's game on, woman. But don't say I didn't warn you."

Julie stuck out her chin, egging him on. Then she screamed as Max smeared mud on her shoulders and chest, his palms grazing the front of her shirt.

"Now look what you've done," cried Julie, in exaggerated dismay. She looked down at her muddy shirt. "What a mess. I can't wear this."

Feeling bold and daring, Julie peeled off her shirt, stripping down to her tank top. She tossed the shirt down the bank.

In the manner of someone getting down to business, Max likewise pulled off his sodden outer shirt, revealing a white T-shirt underneath. He wadded up his shirt and flung it aside.

Suddenly Julie realized that they weren't engaged in a childish game anymore. This was man and woman play, the sort of roughhousing that erupts between two people who can't keep their hands off each other for another second.

There was a sense of excitement in the air, as taut and tense as a tightrope. Julie felt a clenching of animal attraction in the pit of her stomach. Her gaze slid across Max's chest, its manly contours revealed in outline through the thin cotton of his T-shirt. Her heart skipped a beat.

"I know what you need," she said, tossing Max a flirtatious, sideways glance.

"Oh, yeah?" he said, his voice a low rumble and his eyes locked on hers. "What do I need?"

"This!" said Julie.

With that, she leaned forward on her knees and splayed her muddy hands across Max's chest, leaving two brown handprints on his T-shirt. Then she dragged her hands along his neck, marking his skin with muddy finger streaks.

Roaring like a bull, Max lunged at Julie and grabbed her by the wrists. Then he threw himself on her and pinned her to the ground with one of his legs thrown across her lower body.

Squealing and struggling, Julie managed to wriggle free. Panting for breath, her chest rising and falling, she tossed back her hair and gave Max a challenging smile.

"Oh, no, you don't," said Max, grasping one of Julie's ankles as she tried to crawl away.

Julie laughed and screamed again as Max pulled her to him, sliding her across the mud on her back.

When she reached Max, Julie rose to her knees and tried to topple him backward.

But Max was ready for her this time. He wrapped his arms around her, trapping her in a bear hug, and wrestled her into submission. Then they rolled together down the slope, coming to rest at the bottom.

They lay there panting for a moment or two. Max's body

rested on top of Julie's, with his weight on his elbows. He held Julie's gaze for a heartbeat or two, and then he lowered his lips to hers.

Their kiss was long and unhurried, a sweet melding of tenderness and the insistent heat of mutual attraction.

Julie twined her arms around Max, eagerly molding her body to his and returning his kiss. With her whole being, she was instinctively opening up to him like a flower.

When their mouths finally parted, Max pressed his lips to Julie's brow and whispered in her ear.

"I can't tell you how much I've wanted to do this," he said, his voice a husky murmur as his hand caressed Julie's cheek. "Thinking about holding you like this has been driving me crazy."

He nuzzled her throat, imprinting her skin with a string of kisses that made Julie's knees go weak. She'd never in her life felt so drawn to a man, so utterly lost in his embrace.

"Max," she whispered, and sought his lips.

Their kiss lasted longer this time, its intensity matching the pounding of Julie's heart. She closed her eyes, registering only the touch of Max's lips on hers and the sound of their breathing, almost as one.

Julie opened her eyes as Max kissed her brow and the side of her face.

"Even with mud on your cheek," said Max, chuckling deep in his throat, "you're adorable."

Julie smiled and reached her arm around Max, pulling him to her. Then she stopped, her body suddenly going stiff with alarm.

"What is it?" murmured Max, reacting to the change in her. He looked into her eyes and gently brushed back her hair.

"My-my ring," said Julie, stammering in dismay. She was looking at her left hand, which was draped around Max's neck. "I've lost my ring."

She rolled away from Max and sat up. She looked around,

her eyes frantically searching the ground for her wedding band.

"Maybe you left it in your cabin," said Max, rising to his knees. He leaned back on his heels, his hands resting on his thighs. His cheeks carried a now-fading flush. "Are you sure you had it on?"

"I *never* take it off," said Julie, fighting an upwelling of panic. She began groping around in the mud with her fingers. "It must have slipped off when you and I were—"

She stopped, suddenly feeling self-conscious and a little bit guilty. How could she have allowed herself to engage in horseplay with Max—and then return his embraces, kiss for kiss—while still wearing the golden symbol of her marriage to Simon? She almost wept with remorse.

"Where's my ring?" she said, her voice breaking.

"Take it easy," said Max, laying a calming hand on her shoulder. "It's here somewhere. Come on, I'll help you find it."

Together they searched the ground on their hands and knees, looking for a telltale lump in the mud or the glint of gold.

Finally, Max called out. "I found it," he said, holding up the wedding band. "Here's your ring, Julie."

"Thank goodness," cried Julie, rushing over to him.

She took the ring from him and wiped it clean. She started to put the ring back on her finger, when Max gently stayed her hand.

"Julie, wait," he said.

Julie looked up into Max's eyes, trying to read what was there.

"What is it?" she said.

"Don't you think it's time?" said Max, speaking in a quiet voice. He cupped the side of Julie's face with his palm and leaned forward to softly kiss her lips.

"What do you mean?" she asked, but she'd already guessed what Max was asking of her.

"I think a part of you," he said, "is still living in the past,

Julie. You said yourself that your husband would want you to move on." He nodded toward the ring. "So, don't you think it's time to stop wearing that?"

Julie gazed up at him and understood his message. Max was staking his claim on her emotions. And he was asking her to take a stand and shift into the present.

She hesitated. Then, feeling grateful for Max's nudge in the right direction, she mutely nodded and slipped the ring into one of her pockets. She closed the zipper on the pocket, blinked away a little rush of tears, and gave Max a tremulous smile.

Julie felt a tidal wave of emotion sweep over her. She knew that this was the end of an era, the closing of a personal chapter. She'd remember that chapter, her years with Simon, for the rest of her life. But she could now look forward without regret. Although she'd keep Simon's ring as a precious memento of their time together, that symbolic circle of gold would never again be on her finger.

Max seemed to sense the emotions that were rocking Julie's soul. He gathered her in his arms and drew her close.

Julie knew that Max was respecting her need to connect with her innermost feelings. He offered neither advice nor solutions. He simply held her, stroking her hair and silently communicating his support, giving Julie a chance to sort out her thoughts and compose herself.

"We should probably get going," he said presently, glancing up at the position of the sun. It was midafternoon by then. "Let's wash off."

"What's next on our busy schedule?" said Julie, focusing her mind back on business.

"We're going into the forest with Noelle," said Max. "She wants me to take some pictures of her at an ant swarm, for a presentation back at her university. We'll go find an ant swarm with her."

"An ant swarm?" said Julie. She rubbed her arms and gave a little shiver. "Oh, boy, does that ever sound creepy-crawly."

"Yeah, I know," said Max, smiling, "but ant swarms are great. You won't believe your eyes. An ant swarm is one of the most dramatic events in the rain forest. Trust me, you're going to be impressed by what you see."

"If you say so," said Julie, sounding doubtful.

Max went up the bank to fetch Julie's bundle of leaves and flowers. He placed the plant bundle in the boat, retrieved their discarded shirts, and then joined Julie at the water's edge. They rinsed their shirts, rung them out, and tossed them into the boat.

Next, they waded into the river in their clothes to clean the rest of the mud from themselves and from their garments. As they laughed and splashed each other like two playful otters, their earlier lighthearted mood returned. And, as before, their play soon evolved into something else.

Max pulled his wet T-shirt over his head, his well-formed biceps flexing, and threw it into the boat. Now bare from the waist up, he caught Julie's wrist and pulled her to him in the proprietary way of a man who reaches for what he wants.

Julie found Max's male self-confidence very appealing, and she allowed herself to be drawn into his embrace. She placed her palms against his warm, wet chest. His skin was smooth, his muscles firm and solid. She recalled the figure study she'd drawn of him, based on what she'd guessed his naked chest might look like. The reality, she found, was much better than what her imagination had conjured.

She also discovered that Max had told the truth about one of the details in her sketch. He *did* have a bit more hair on his chest than she'd drawn. It was just the right amount, concluded Julie.

A minute or two pulsed by as Max and Julie stood in the waist-deep water, kissing with their arms wrapped around each other. Finally, Julie broke the delicious contact of their lips and spoke.

"Noelle's going to send out a search party," she said, with a laugh, "if you and I don't show up at the station pretty soon."

"Yeah, you're right," said Max, cupping Julie's face in his hands and kissing her one more time. "Ant swarms are the farthest thing from my mind at the moment," he added, his voice low and husky against her throat, "but we'd better get going."

Hand in hand, they waded to the boat. Max lifted Julie over the gunwale. Then he untied the line and pushed on the bow, easing the boat off the sandbar.

He climbed aboard, used a paddle to guide the boat into the main current, and then started the engine. Soon they were motoring back down the river, the emerald-green rain forest gliding by on either side.

"Hear that?" said Max, keeping his voice low as he spoke to Julie.

"You mean," said Julie, whispering, "those soft, trilling noises?"

Max nodded.

"What's making those sounds?" she said, trying to penetrate the dim light of the rain forest with her eyes.

"Those are antbirds," said Noelle, who was standing nearby. She grinned at Max and Julie. "Their calls are going to lead us straight to an ant swarm."

It was late afternoon of the same day. Julie, Max, and Noelle had hiked into the forest on one of the trails, searching for army ants on a hunting raid. Now they left the trail and followed the excited calls of the antbirds. They tied orange markers every few yards as they went, a precaution against becoming lost.

"Aren't army ants dangerous?" asked Julie, as the three of them wove their way through the trees.

"Only to their prey," said Noelle, "which includes pretty much anything they can stir up—insects, snakes, spiders, even small mammals—as they swarm through the forest."

"Do antbirds eat ants?" said Julie.

"No, they don't," said Max, as he tied a strip of orange plastic to a bush. "They're called antbirds because they travel along with the swarm, eating the *insects* that the ants stir up. There are usually several species of antbird working the same swarm, picking off insects as they go."

"Oh, I see," said Julie, nodding. "But what about us? Won't the ants crawl up our legs?"

"That's why we're wearing these," said Max, indicating the knee-high rubber boots all three of them had on. "The ants will crawl over our feet, but not up our boots." He smiled at her. "Don't worry, I haven't been bitten yet."

They walked for another minute or so, homing in on the mellow chirping of the antbirds. Presently, Max held up his hand and they halted.

"Okay, we're getting close," he whispered, and took a camera out of his knapsack. "Let's creep forward a few more yards." He put a finger to his lips. "Quiet, everyone."

Julie, Max, and Noelle slowly moved through the understory, pausing now and then to glance around and get their bearings. Soon they reached the outer edge of the army ants' hunting raid.

Julie caught her breath and stared in wonder. She'd never seen anything like this in her life. The forest floor itself seemed to be alive. It undulated with activity as a river of ants flowed over every leaf, twig, and stone. A soft, rustling sound filled the air, created by the scurrying footfalls of half a million ants.

"I can't believe this," said Julie, whispering in Max's ear. "It's the most amazing thing I've ever seen."

"Look over there," said Max, indicating the leading edge of the swarm. "See the antbirds?"

"Oh, yes," said Julie, as she spotted a dozen or so dark-colored birds of various species. Smaller than robins, the antbirds were hopping and darting about as they snapped up insects fleeing from the ants. "This is so interesting," she added, and squeezed Max's arm.

He smiled back at her, obviously pleased by her reaction.

Betsy Rogers

For the next half hour, Julie, Max, and Noelle kept pace with the swarm, sometimes crouching near the ground to get a better look. Max took pictures of Noelle in the thick of the action, documenting her field studies as an ant specialist.

Later, back at the station, they all went their separate ways. Noelle went to the library, Max disappeared into his study to catch up on paperwork, and Julie went to her cabin intending to shower and change before dinner.

At her cabin, Julie discovered that she needed a fresh towel. Walking over to the main building, she located Hernando's wife Isabel, who was in charge of housekeeping, in the laundry room.

Isabel was a short, brown-skinned woman with broad cheeks and glossy, black braids. She spoke broken English.

"Hello, Isabel," said Julie, as she entered the laundry room.

"*Hola,* Senorita Julie," said Isabel, smiling. She paused at her task of folding clean linens into a basket. "How may I help you?"

"I just need a towel," said Julie. "Thanks," she added, as Isabel fetched her one from a shelf.

As Julie turned to leave, something interesting caught her eye. She walked over to the table where Isabel was working and picked up a cloth with colorful embroidery around the edges.

"Did you do this stitching, Isabel?" asked Julie.

"No," said Isabel, shaking her head. "Is made by my friend Maria who live in the village."

"You mean, Laguna Miguel?" said Julie, inspecting the piece of fabric, which was the size of a small tablecloth.

"*Sí,*" said Isabel, nodding.

"This is beautiful," said Julie, appraising the work with an artist's eye. She'd always admired quality handwork. "The stitching is neat and precise, and the design is so unusual." She regarded Isabel. "Do you have any more like this?"

"*Sí,*" said Isabel.

Walking over to a cupboard, Isabel brought out several more

tablecloths and matching sets of napkins. She placed them on the table for Julie to look at.

"These are incredible," said Julie, shaking out one of the tablecloths and holding it up. "Each one has a different border design, I notice."

"This one is flowers," said Isabel, pointing to one of the cloths. "And this one is butterflies." She smiled, the corners of her eyes crinkling. "Many kinds of forest plants and animals."

"I see that," said Julie, sorting through the pile. "These are like embroidered nature studies." She paused. "Oh, here's one of birds," she said, running her hand over one of the cloths. "This stitching is so realistic and so full of detail." She looked at Isabel. "Your friend Maria is very talented."

"Oh," said Isabel, "a different woman made that one." She riffled through the pile. "These all made by different women."

"Wow," said Julie, as the information sank in. "Are you saying that *several* women in the village can stitch like this?"

"*Sí*," said Isabel, nodding, "many women in the village do this handwork. It is—how do you say?—a tradition in Laguna Miguel." She patted the pile. "Perhaps I take these to Cuzco someday to sell for the women."

"Hmm," said Julie, as an idea began forming in her mind. "Has Doctor Max seen any of these?"

"I don't think so," said Isabel, shaking her head.

"May I borrow this one?" asked Julie, indicating the tablecloth with the stitched birds. "I'd like to show it to him."

"Of course," said Isabel, gesturing with her hands. "Please, take it with you."

As Julie left the laundry room with the tablecloth tucked under her arm, she was barely able to contain her excitement. Instead of returning to her cabin, she made a beeline for Max's study, so that she could show him the tablecloth.

Julie smiled to herself, marveling at the mysterious ways of serendipity. By chance, she'd stumbled onto something that had enormous potential. Through their imaginative stitching, the talented craftswomen of Laguna Miguel had given Julie an idea.

She believed that, with a little creative thinking, the women's artistry might be used to build a cooperative bridge between Max and the Pierson-Roth plan. As a wonderful bonus, such a bridge would also generate income for the village.

As Julie mounted the outside steps to Max's study, she mentally crossed her fingers. This might be the breakthrough she'd been hoping for. Could she convince Max that her idea was worth considering? Or would he dismiss it as too far-fetched?

The latter seemed more likely, but there was only one way to find out. Taking a deep breath, Julie knocked on Max's door.

Chapter Nine

Julie knocked a second time on the door to Max's study.

"Come in," Max called out, from within.

Julie turned the knob and entered, closing the door behind her. She found Max sitting at his desk, working at his laptop. An air of concentration surrounded him, punctuated by the sound of the clicking of computer keys.

"Oh, hi, Julie," said Max, glancing her way. "Have a seat. I'm almost done here."

Julie sat on a chair near Max's desk. She held the tablecloth she'd borrowed from Isabel on her lap, folded so that the embroidered birds were hidden from view.

She was bursting to show Max the tablecloth. But she wanted to share her plan with him first and try to arouse his curiosity, before revealing the beautiful needlework that had inspired her idea.

She studied Max's profile, trying to judge his mood. She was hoping that he was in a receptive frame of mind, but it was hard to tell just by looking at him. He seemed hard at work at the moment, his brow creased in thought as his fingers flew over the keyboard. When he finally clicked SEND and, with a sigh, sat back in his chair, Julie knew he'd been composing an e-mail.

"Okay, *that's* done," he said, and swept his fingers through his hair.

Julie could tell that Max was preoccupied, his mind clearly somewhere else. Perhaps she should put off sharing her idea with him until the next morning.

"What's up, Julie?" asked Max, swiveling his chair to face in her direction.

"You know," she said, "I think I've caught you at a bad time." She started to rise from her chair. "I want to talk to you about something, but it can wait until tomorrow."

"Don't go," said Max, motioning for her to stay. "I won't be here tomorrow, so let's talk now."

"You won't be here?" said Julie, feeling thrown off balance by this unexpected news.

"No, something's come up," said Max, "and I have to leave for Lima early in the morning." He nodded toward his computer. "That e-mail I just sent was in answer to a colleague of mine, agreeing to do him a favor."

"A favor?"

"Yeah, he was supposed to speak at a biodiversity conference in Lima this week," said Max, "but he's had to cancel at the last minute. He's asked me to go in his place, and I've told him I would."

"That's nice of you," said Julie. She admired Max's generosity, yet she felt let down at the thought of his leaving.

"He hasn't given me much lead time," said Max, with a wry laugh, "but these things can happen." He gave an oh-well kind of shrug. "Besides, he'd do the same for me."

"Hmm," said Julie, nodding. Then she added, "How long will you be gone?"

"About ten days," said Max. He pointed toward a stack of manila file folders. "Somehow I've got to pull a couple of presentations out of all that material." He gave a rueful shake of his head. "What have I gotten myself into? I'll be up half the night."

"Well, I should leave you to it," said Julie, standing up.

"But don't you want to tell me something?"

"Yes, but it can wait. Really, it can. You're too busy right now."

"Not *that* busy," said Max, smiling in a way that warmed Julie's heart.

He reached for her wrist and pulled her down to sit on his lap. He wrapped his arms around her waist and planted a kiss on her bare shoulder.

Julie looked into Max's eyes. "It won't be the same around here without you," she said. She traced his cheek with her fingers. "We're all going to miss you. *I'm* going to miss you."

"I'm going to miss you too," said Max, his voice laced with hidden, heartfelt meaning. "I'd much rather stay here than go all the way to Lima, but I kind of owe that friend of mine a favor. Still, the timing is terrible." He nuzzled Julie's neck, his breath as warm as honey on her skin. "You and I were just getting to know each other."

They embraced in silence for a moment or two. Then Max said, "Now, what's on your mind, Julie?"

"I want to show you something," said Julie, returning to her chair, "but first I want to tell you about an idea I've had."

"Okay," said Max, leaning back in his chair to listen. He regarded her. "Does this have something to do with Pierson-Roth, by any chance?"

"In a way."

"Hmm, I thought it might," said Max, not sounding pleased.

"Well, it is my job," said Julie. "I'm their representative, so just hear me out, okay?"

Max gestured for her to go on.

"What if I were to tell you," said Julie, launching into the little speech she'd been mentally rehearsing, "that I've thought of a way for Laguna Miguel to earn money off tourism, even though the tourists would stay here, at the station, instead of in the village?"

"I've suggested a compromise," said Max, with a frown of impatience. "You and I have already been over this ground."

"Yes, we've thrown some ideas around," said Julie. "And I've prepared you for the fact that having visitors stay at the village is probably not practical." She regarded Max. "I'll have some final figures for you by the time you get back from Lima."

He nodded.

"But in the meantime," said Julie, "I want you to consider this. There are many ways you can help Laguna Miguel."

She began ticking off items on her fingers.

"You can pay men from the village to build some tourist cabins at Manu River," she said. "You can hire service personnel from the village to work here. And you can hire and train local guides to take visitors into the forest."

She leaned forward in her chair.

"Think about it, Max. You'll create jobs, you'll help the village, and the tourists who are going to flock to Manu River—"

"What makes you think they'll *flock* here?" said Max, interrupting her.

"Because I'm going to design an attractive Web page for you," said Julie. "Once the word gets out, people will come. I'm sure of it."

Max cast his eyes toward the ceiling for a moment, clearly unmoved by Julie's enthusiasm.

"But, wait, there's more," said Julie, still giving her pitch. "Look at this, Max."

With that, she rose from her chair, unfolded the tablecloth, and held it up for him to see.

"What's this?" said Max, staring at the cloth with a puzzled look on his face.

"This," said Julie, "is an example of some talented stitching that's being done right under our noses."

"Where'd you get this?" said Max, his gaze running along the border of embroidered birds.

"I borrowed it from Isabel," said Julie. "It was made by hand in Laguna Miguel. And there's a lot more where this came from."

Max said nothing.

"Now, here's my plan," she continued. "I'd like to help set up a little gift shop at Manu River, where the village women can sell their needlework and other crafts. The women would make money, and Manu River would get a percentage of the profits. It's a win-win situation."

"I don't want tourists staying here," said Max, sounding beleaguered.

"I'm aware of that," said Julie, "but you might have to bend on that point, especially if the figures add up the way I think they're going to."

She paused.

"In any case," she added, "the board of directors at Pierson-Roth will have the last say. Once I submit my report, the decision will be out of both your hands and mine."

Max sighed.

"You know what I think?" said Julie.

"What?"

"I predict," she said, "that the board will instruct that cabins be built here, and that your dining facility be expanded to accommodate guests. If those changes don't take place, there's a good chance that Manu River will be closed altogether."

"I can't let that happen," said Max, passing a hand over his brow.

"It doesn't have to happen," said Julie. "Look, I know you don't support the tourist idea right now, but it won't be the end of the world. You'll continue to carry out the scientific mission of the station as your number-one priority. And, as I've said, the renovation will create jobs for the villagers. You'll be helping

Laguna Miguel, just not exactly in the way you thought you would be."

Max stared into space, his expression that of a man feeling hemmed in on all sides.

"Face it, Max," said Julie, speaking with kindly diplomacy, "change is coming to Manu River. You may as well be part of it."

Still he said nothing.

"Tell me what you're thinking," said Julie, attempting to read the look on his face. "I'm trying to come up with a plan that will cover all the bases. And you're going to need that plan if my figures prove that Manu River has to generate revenue through tourism."

There was another long, uncomfortable pause.

"Oh, I've thought of something else," said Julie, determined to forge ahead. "I could design some Manu River T-shirts, which could also be sold in the gift shop."

"T-shirts?" said Max, sounding as if the word left a bad taste in his mouth.

"That's right," said Julie, ignoring his tone. "You know, with an attractive logo and a painting of a bird on the front. Travelers love buying T-shirts. They're good souvenirs, and they make great gifts for friends back home."

She regarded Max.

"I'd be happy to do the paintings for the shirts," she added. "Subject to your approval, of course."

"Well," said Max, expelling his breath, "you've certainly given this a lot of thought."

"Just trying to help," said Julie. "And, honestly, what do you think of this needlework?" she asked, draping the bottom edge of the tablecloth across his knees. "It's gorgeous, isn't it?"

"I don't know the first thing about sewing," said Max, fingering the cloth, "but even I can see that this is beautiful work."

"And did you notice," said Julie, "that these are not simply caricatures of birds? These have been stitched with such accuracy that they look like actual, identifiable species. At least they do to me." She pointed to one of the birds. "Isn't this a mustached wren, like the one we caught in the mist net?"

"Yes," said Max, nodding, "it's a perfect likeness of a mustached wren." He studied the cloth with greater interest. "I have to say, this is remarkable. Whoever created this is very observant."

"Isabel told me," said Julie, "that embroidery is a tradition in Laguna Miguel. Apparently most of the women in the village can do this kind of work."

"Hmm."

"So, tell me what species these are," said Julie, referring to the tablecloth. Inside, she was rejoicing at having sparked Max's curiosity.

"Well, let's see," said Max, running his hand along the row of birds. "Here we have a barred antshrike, and that one's a masked tityra. This is a buff-throated woodcreeper," he continued, going from bird to bird, "and the next one is a—"

He stopped.

"Go on," said Julie. "What's that one called?"

"It's not called anything," said Max, with a little headshake. "There's no such bird."

"Are you sure?" asked Julie.

"Of course I'm sure," said Max, with the quiet confidence of an expert. "I'm writing a field guide for Manu National Park, remember? I've researched every single ornithological study that's come out of this part of Peru—in addition to my own data, of course—and I'm telling you there's no such bird as this."

"Well, you should know," said Julie, acknowledging his expertise.

"I'd darn well better know," said Max, laughing. He returned his gaze to the cloth. "But except for that one, all of these others are absolutely true to life."

"Hmm," said Julie, thinking. "Why do you suppose whoever

stitched this portrayed all these real birds and then threw in one that's completely made-up?"

"I have no idea," said Max. "Besides, it doesn't really matter. It's the artistry that counts." He shrugged. "So what if it's a made-up bird? I'm guessing that people who buy this kind of work don't care one way or the other."

"Wouldn't it be something, though," said Julie, still puzzling over the question, "if this were a brand-new species?"

"You mean," said Max, "a bird that hasn't been discovered yet by the scientific community?"

"That's right," said Julie, gazing at the mystery bird. "Maybe the locals know about this bird, but scientists have somehow overlooked it."

"That's very unlikely," said Max. "This part of Peru has been studied up one side and down the other, including the area around Laguna Miguel. If there were a bird out there like this," he said, tapping the cloth, "one of us would've noticed it by now."

"Hmm."

"Now, if this *were* a real species," said Max, "I'd certainly like to see it for myself." He studied the mystery bird. "It looks a bit like a *Grallaria,*" he added, musing to himself.

"What's that?" asked Julie.

"*Grallarias* are a type of antpitta," said Max. "They're generally robin-sized or smaller, with long legs and short tails. A lot of *Grallaria* species hop around on the ground, foraging for food."

Julie nodded.

"The bird on this cloth," continued Max, "could almost be *Grallaria eludens,* except for this broad, speckled band across the back." He shook his head. "But there's no such antpitta as this. Here, I'll show you."

With that, he reached into a drawer and pulled out a file containing photographs of birds. He riffled through the file and then handed one of the photos to Julie.

"That's a picture of *Grallaria eludens*," he said, tapping the photo.

"Oh, I see what you mean," said Julie, gazing at the image. It showed a bird with a pale chest and dark wings and back. "The bird on the tablecloth *does* look like this one, except for the addition of the speckled band across the back."

"That's the key word," said Max, "*addition*. Whoever embroidered that cloth probably had *Grallaria eludens* in mind. Then, on a whim, she added the speckled band."

"In other words," said Julie, "she took artistic license."

"Yep."

"Well, I can identify with that."

"Yes, I'm sure you can," said Max, amusement tugging at the corners of his mouth. "After all, aren't you the artist who goes around portraying fully clothed men with their shirts off?"

Julie felt her cheeks grow warm, but she laughed all the same. She didn't mind in the least that Max felt free to tease her about her so-called "figure study" of him.

"Yes, what we have here," continued Max, his eyes returning to the mystery bird, "is a case of artistic license, which is something we scientists are not allowed to indulge in, I'm afraid." He tucked the photo back into the file. "Like I said, there's no such bird as the one on that cloth."

"What's the common name for the bird in the photo?" asked Julie.

"Elusive antpitta."

"Meaning it's hard to see?"

"That's right," said Max, nodding. "Antpittas are generally hard to find."

"Why is that?"

"Because they tend to stay hidden in dense foliage," said Max, "and they quietly skulk around like mice. They're *all* frustratingly elusive." He shrugged. "Sometimes the only way to see an antpitta is to coax it out with a taped recording of its call."

"How does that work?"

"You play a tape of their call," explained Max, "and when they hear it, they pop out to investigate. If you're lucky, you get a quick look at the bird before it vanishes back into the brush."

There was a long pause.

"If antpittas are that hard to see," said Julie, thinking out loud, "isn't it possible that the one on the tablecloth has been overlooked?"

"Oh, I suppose," said Max, his tone revealing that he was losing interest in the subject, "but it's extremely unlikely."

"You know," said Julie, smiling, "scientists aren't the only ones with eyes in the forest."

"That is true," said Max, giving a good-natured laugh. "Tell you what. If you find one of those speckle-backed antpittas, take me to it, okay? It's not every day that I get to clap eyes on a brand-new species. But," he added, with emphasis, "I won't hold my breath."

Julie nodded as she refolded the cloth.

"Now let's table our discussion of imaginary birds," said Max, "and get personal for a minute."

Julie sat on her chair, facing Max.

Max moved his chair toward her, so that their knees touched. Then he took both of her hands in his.

Julie's heart skipped a beat as she looked into Max's eyes. He had such an earnest expression on his face. What did he want to say to her?

"Julie," he began, "I want to talk about us."

"What about us?" said Julie, feeling her pulse accelerate.

"Do you remember my saying," said Max, "that I wished we'd met under different circumstances?"

"Yes."

"When I first saw you," he said, "I was immediately attracted." He reached out and gently touched her cheek. "I still am, more than ever."

"I feel the same way," said Julie, speaking in a quiet voice.

"I'm attracted to you too." Her heart sang to say those words out loud.

"But I knew at the beginning," continued Max, "that I should keep my feelings to myself, because I could see that you were wearing a wedding band." He gave a little shrug. "I just naturally assumed that you had a husband waiting for you back home."

Julie nodded, picturing the gold ring that was now tucked away in her cabin. Her ring finger felt naked without it, but she knew that, with time, she would get used to the change. An era had passed. It was Julie's turn to move on.

"When I learned that you were no longer married," Max went on, "well, a door opened." He grazed her lips with his. "Still, I must admit that it's frustrating to me that we're on opposite sides of this Pierson-Roth business." He gave a rueful shake of his head. "The idea of tourism encroaching on Manu River is tearing me apart."

"I know," said Julie, watching a flame of combat briefly flare in Max's eyes.

"Which is why," he continued, "I wish we'd met in a completely different context. Being on opposing sides of that issue is a complication I'd rather do without." He paused. "But I obviously have to live with it."

Julie listened, saying nothing but simply letting Max air his thoughts.

"I know you're only doing what you were hired for," said Max, "and I can appreciate that. You're trying to do your best."

He expelled his breath.

"You've even come up with ideas that you think will work— T-shirts, Web sites, the hiring of a manager for the tourism end of things, and so forth." He gazed into Julie's eyes. "You're very creative, and I admire that about you."

"I just think it's important," said Julie, "that Manu River becomes more self-supporting. I want the research station to stay open too, you know."

"Yes, I believe you do," said Max. "But why can't we agree on the basic plan? Why must we keep butting heads over that?"

"That's just the way things happen to be," said Julie, feeling helpless to explain their situation in any other terms. "Things are what they are."

"Yeah," said Max, acknowledging her philosophical point of view, "things are what they are."

He cupped her face in his hands.

"Well, here's what I really want to say to you, Julie Winlock," he went on. "We may not agree on what's best for Manu River. But could we at least agree not to let those differences come between us?"

"Of course we can, Max," said Julie, putting her arms around his neck and kissing him.

When their lips parted, there was a long, thoughtful pause.

"You know," said Max, breaking the silence, "I really hate to leave Manu River right now." He leaned back a little to regard Julie. "Ten days is a long while."

"I was thinking that too."

"The timing's not good at all," said Max, shaking his head. "You and I were just getting to know each other, and now I have to leave." He paused. "But here's an idea. Why don't you come with me, Julie?"

"You mean, to Lima?" she said, his invitation taking her by surprise.

"Sure," said Max, smiling. "You're still officially shadowing me, aren't you?"

"Well, yes, but . . ." Her voice trailed off.

"So shadow me to Lima," he said. "We'll travel on your terms, of course," he added, hastening to reassure her. "We can have separate rooms, if that's what you want, and we'll be all business. Well, maybe not *all* business," he amended, with a twinkle in his eye. "We'll have some fun too."

Julie said nothing for a moment, but her mind was in a whirl.

Max's offer was tempting. She hadn't seen much of Lima, so briefly had she passed through there on her way to Manu River, via Cuzco. What she'd glimpsed from the taxi that whisked her from the airport to the train station, however, had whetted her appetite to return sometime and do some sightseeing.

Exploring Lima, that beautiful city on the Pacific Coast, sounded appealing, especially if Max were with her. But Julie had mixed feelings about the timing of his invitation.

"You're going to like Lima," said Max, enthusiastically pitching his idea. "It has wonderful cathedrals and art museums, and you'll love the outdoor markets. While I'm at the conference during the day, you can wander around and sketch to your heart's content."

"That would be fun," said Julie, thinking it over.

"Then in the evening," continued Max, "I'll take you wining and dining. Lima has some excellent restaurants that serve authentic Peruvian food. One of my favorite places is the Ambrosia, at Hotel Miraflores. You'd love the Ambrosia."

Julie listened, her interest definitely piqued. She knew that Max would be the perfect companion on a trip to Lima. She could picture the two of them seated at a table romantically aglow with candles, the surrounding walls decorated with Incan Indian motifs. Afterward, they could stroll hand in hand through moonlit plazas decked with gardens and statuary. Oh, yes, such a trip, with Max by her side, would be wonderful beyond description.

"Think of it this way," said Max, interrupting her thoughts. "Spending time together in Lima would give us a chance to get to know each other better."

"I do like that idea," said Julie, nodding in agreement.

"We'd have so much fun," said Max, his eyes lighting up with happy anticipation. "If there's time," he added, "we'll take a side trip to Machu Picchu. I'd love to show you those ancient ruins."

"Machu Picchu," breathed Julie, recalling pictures she'd seen of that legendary Inca stronghold, dramatically surrounded by steep mountains. "I've always wanted to go there."

"So come with me," urged Max, squeezing her hand. "Say you will, Julie."

Julie felt a pang of guilt. Max was gazing at her with such a naked look of hope and enthusiasm on his face that she hated to let him down. But she knew she must.

"I'm really tempted," she began. "It's nice of you to ask me, but I can't go with you."

"Of course you can," said Max, his happy expression fading around the edges. "What's holding you back?"

"I have a job to do, Max."

"But we'll only be gone for ten days," he said, still trying to persuade her. He gave a wave of his hand. "The business with Pierson-Roth will still be here when we come back. It can wait."

"No, I don't think it can," said Julie. "I can't tell you how much I'd love to go traveling with you. You make all of it sound so wonderful."

"We'd have a great time."

"I know," said Julie, nodding, "but I truly believe that my place is here right now. Pierson-Roth hired me to do a job. I should stay focused on that task until there's some kind of resolution. Please try and understand."

Max's silence spoke volumes. He was clearly disappointed by Julie's decision.

"I'm sorry to let you down," said Julie, laying her hand on Max's arm. "But it's best that I stay here and work on my report. The sooner I submit my findings to the Foundation, the sooner we'll all know what the future holds for Manu River. If I went to Lima with you, I'd just be putting off the inevitable."

She paused.

"And to be honest," she went on, "I think I'd be too distracted on our trip, thinking about the work still waiting for me back here. I'm sure I wouldn't be able to enjoy myself the way I'd like to."

"Hmm."

"The first time I see Machu Picchu," said Julie, laughing, "I don't want my mind cluttered with financial spreadsheets and cost projections." She looked into Max's eyes. "Please say you understand."

There was a long pause. Then Max gave a brief nod and pressed Julie's hand.

"I do," he said. "I won't say I'm not disappointed, but I can understand your position. You're very conscientious, Julie. Pierson-Roth hired the right person."

Julie smiled.

"I would have loved having your company," said Max, "but this is probably for the best. You stay here and write your report." He leaned forward to kiss her. "Lima and Machu Picchu will still be there when you finish. Maybe we can see them together some other time."

"Thank you, Max," said Julie, grateful that he recognized the importance in her remaining behind. "I'll make a lot of progress over the next ten days. By the time you get back, I'll have some final figures to share with you, and you'll have a much clearer picture of Manu River's future."

"Right," said Max, lifting her hand to kiss her wrist. Then he stirred in his chair. "Well, I suppose I should get cracking on those presentations for the conference."

"I'll take that as a hint," said Julie, laughing. She rose from her seat and tucked the embroidered tablecloth under her arm. "Will I see you in the morning before you leave?" she asked.

"Not unless you plan to get up before dawn," said Max, already sorting through the mountain of file folders on his desk. He shot her a smile. "Sleep in, Julie. You've earned it."

"Have a safe trip, Max," said Julie.

"Thanks," said Max. "Oh, and keep your eyes peeled while I'm gone," he added, teasing her. "You know, just in case the imaginary antpitta on that cloth hops out in front of you." He chuckled as he opened one of the folders.

"You know," said Julie, rising to the bait, "I have half a mind to go to Laguna Miguel and search for that bird myself."

"You do that," said Max, distracted by his work.

"I was planning on going there anyway," continued Julie, thinking out loud. "I may as well ask around about the mystery bird while I'm there."

"Tell you what," said Max, removing a staple from some papers, "if you find such a bird, I'll eat my hat."

"I have a better idea," said Julie, as an audacious plan popped into her mind. "Let's make a deal."

"What kind of deal?" he asked, reaching for a yellow highlighter.

"If I can prove that there really *is* such a bird—"

"Not going to happen," said Max, with irritating complacency as he began marking one of the pages with the highlighter.

"But if I *can* prove it," said Julie, forging ahead, "I want you to agree to something."

"And what would that be?" said Max, his eyes on the page.

"If that bird turns out to be real," said Julie, "I want you to let some ecotourists come here for a trial visit."

That got Max's full attention. His hand with the marker stopped moving across the page and his head came up. He regarded her.

"There's *no such bird*, Julie," he said, with emphasis.

"But I have a hunch about it," she said, trying to sound more sure of herself than she actually felt.

"Hunches don't count," said Max, returning to his work. "You should leave science to the scientists. There's no such bird."

Julie bit back a sharp retort.

"But you know what?" he went on. "I'm happy to agree to your deal. If you can offer me proof that there's a so-called speckle-backed antpitta somewhere out there, I'll let you bring in some tourists on a trial visit."

"Just to be clear," said Julie, "I'm talking about *overnight* visitors."

"Sure, why not?" said Max, chuckling. "There's no place for them to sleep, and our dining hall isn't set up to feed a crowd of people. But hey," he continued, with an airy wave of his hand, "don't let those minor details stop you."

"I think I recognize sarcasm when I hear it," commented Julie, one hand on her hip. "You know, it would serve you right if I did find that bird."

"Yes, I suppose it would," said Max, undeterred. He reached for another folder. "But that isn't going to happen and we both know it." He shrugged. "Anyway, I've agreed to your deal."

"Thank you," said Julie, mentally recomposing herself. "Now, that wasn't so hard, was it?"

"Not hard at all," said Max, his brows going up in mock innocence. "I'm only agreeing to your plan because I know I have nothing to lose."

Then his expression changed as he rose from his chair and wrapped Julie in his arms.

"What *is* going to be hard," he said, murmuring against her temple, "is being away from you."

They clung to each other for a minute or two and exchanged kisses.

"I should leave you to your work," said Julie, finally stepping away from him. "I'll miss you, Max. Have a safe trip."

Julie let herself out, feeling warmed by Max's embrace but also miffed by some of his remarks. Her thoughts churned as she descended the stairs. She knew that Max was probably right about one thing. The chances of discovering a new bird species were practically zero.

More to the point, even if there were a mystery bird out there, skulking in the underbrush, how could she, a nonscientist, presume to be able to prove its existence?

Julie passed a hand across her brow. She must have been out of her mind to suggest such a thing to Max. No wonder he found her idea laughable. Julie had put herself in a tricky position, no doubt about it.

On the other hand, what if her hunch was right? What if there really was a speckle-backed antpitta out there, just waiting to be discovered? How exciting that would be.

Julie knew that she shouldn't spend valuable time chasing after a bird that probably didn't exist. She ought to be focusing all of her energy on writing her report for Pierson-Roth.

But Max's dismissive attitude had irked her, and Julie felt a need to rise to his challenge. He was so sure of himself, so unwilling to concede that trained scientists were not the only people who could make important discoveries.

Julie walked toward the laundry room, intending to return the tablecloth to Isabel. As she rounded the corner, her thoughts crystallized. She would go to Laguna Miguel, and she would make a few simple inquiries about the mystery bird. There'd be no harm in that.

Besides, the subject would nag at her until she did something about it. Better to confirm that the embroidered mystery bird was the result of artistic license than to continue wondering about it.

And if the bird turned out to be an actual species?

Well, as unlikely as that was, Julie would make the most of such a discovery. She'd paint a portrait of the bird for one of the Manu River T-shirts, and—she had to admit it—she'd enjoy seeing Max eat a little crow.

So to speak.

"Isabel," she called out, pushing open the door to the laundry room. "Are you in here?"

"*Sí.*"

Isabel was sweeping the floor. She put the broom aside as Julie walked over to her and handed her the tablecloth.

"Thanks for letting me borrow this," said Julie. "I showed it to Doctor Max. He was very impressed."

"*Sí,* is very pretty," said Isabel, smiling.

"Tell me," said Julie, "do you have any other pieces with birds on them?"

"I will look," said Isabel.

She went to the cupboard where she kept the needlework. She pulled out the entire pile this time and carried it to a table. Then she and Julie sorted through it together.

"Oh, here's another tablecloth," said Julie, putting that item to one side. "And here are some hand towels with birds on them."

By the time they'd finished, Julie had found eight more pieces of needlework featuring likenesses of birds. The mystery bird appeared on three of them. And, according to Isabel, a different woman had stitched each of the cloths.

"I wonder if this is just a coincidence," murmured Julie, thinking out loud, as she compared the three cloths with the one she'd shown to Max.

Julie knew that, within an artistic community, it was not unheard of for decorative motifs—whether inspired by real or imaginary objects—to be traded back and forth. It was possible, therefore, that one of the seamstresses in Laguna Miguel had used artistic license in stitching an imaginary bird, and that other women had then copied her idea.

Yes, it was likely that what Julie saw spread out on the table was a case of artistic license followed by imitation. Even so, she knew she wouldn't be able to rest until she'd gotten to the bottom of the situation.

Besides, she'd made a deal with Max. And she'd challenged him on the point of who was capable of making new discoveries in the rain forest. Now she felt duty bound to follow through.

Julie frowned to herself. Max's decisive pronouncement—"There's no such bird"—rang in her ears. In his smugness, he probably assumed she wouldn't even try to find out if such a creature existed.

Well, she'd show him.

She picked up a napkin, on which was stitched a picture of the mystery bird, and turned to Isabel.

"May I keep this for a while?" she said.

"Of course," said Isabel.

"Do you know," said Julie, pointing to the stitching, "if there's a bird that actually looks like this?"

Isabel began gathering up the needlework.

"I know nothing about birds," she said, with an apologetic smile. "You will have to ask the women of the village."

She put the needlework back into the cupboard.

"I want to go to Laguna Miguel," said Julie, tucking the napkin into her pocket.

Just then, she remembered something that Max had told her about Cesar, the cook's helper.

"Cesar goes there every week to see his grandmother, doesn't he?"

"*Sí,*" said Isabel, nodding, "you can go in the boat with Cesar. I think he go there in two more days."

"Thanks, Isabel."

Julie left the laundry room and headed for the kitchen, intending to let Cesar know that she wanted to hitch a ride with him to Laguna Miguel. Her mind whirled with plans. Once in the village, she'd talk to the women and ask about the mystery bird that several of them had portrayed in their stitching. Was the speckle-backed antpitta real? Or was it a figment of someone's playful imagination?

Julie knew that her hunch about the bird was a long shot. But even supposing that the bird turned out to be an actual species, was there any chance of her seeing it with her own eyes? The possibility of that happening seemed about as likely as spotting icebergs in the Manu River.

But what if she *did* see the bird? She knew that, in order to convince Max of its authenticity, she'd have to do a lot more than wave a piece of embroidery in his face. And she couldn't just go on hearsay.

No, Max's scientific mind would demand more solid evidence than that. So Julie made a mental note. She would take her sketching pad and her digital camera with her on the trip to Laguna Miguel.

"Just in case," she murmured under her breath, as she approached the kitchen. "Just in case."

Chapter Ten

When is Max getting back?" asked Noelle, at the dinner table.

"Sometime tonight, I think," said Ted. "Pass me those fish tacos, will you, Julie?"

"Here you go," said Julie, handing the platter of tacos to Fran, who then passed it to Ted. Robert snagged another taco and a wedge of lime as the platter went by him.

Julie and the four graduate students were eating an early dinner. It was still light outside. The sun hovered above the horizon, burnishing the tops of the trees before disappearing for the day. The distant call of a howler monkey drifted through the screens, a final declaration of male dominance before the leader and his troop settled in for the night.

An air of anticipation hovered over the table. During the meal, all had said how much they'd missed Max and how glad they'd be to welcome him back. Messages from him had been sketchy during his absence, due to some communication glitches. Now everyone was looking forward to hearing about his trip.

Julie, in particular, was beside herself with excitement. She barely tasted her food as she pictured Max strolling into the room, his eyes searching her out. She could hardly wait to see him.

It seemed like an eternity since Max had left for Lima. The original ten-day trip had extended to a full two weeks, due to "transportation problems," according to Max's most recent message. Now Max was presumed to be on the final leg of his journey home, speeding upriver to the research station.

When Max still hadn't shown up by the time Hernando served dessert, Julie felt a pang of disappointment. Had Max's homecoming been delayed again? Hurrying through her helping of coconut pudding, she excused herself from the table and walked down to the dock to wait.

Light was fading from the sky as Julie stood on the dock, listening intently for the sound of a boat engine. As the minutes crawled by, she began pacing up and down the wooden planks, unable to contain her excitement.

She was eager to talk to Max. Much had happened while he'd been gone, and there'd been some developments. She had a lot of news to share with him, both good and not so good. She fretted over what Max's reaction would be to some of her news. She guessed that he'd be none too pleased.

But Max was a reasonable man and his heart was in the right place. Julie was counting on him to see the benefits in the changes that were coming to his beloved research station. During his time away, he might have thought things through and gained a broader perspective. The ultimate goal, after all, was to save Manu River, even if that meant making bigger compromises than he'd hoped for.

Julie gazed downriver, willing the boat bearing Max back to her to appear around the bend.

She'd kept busy during his absence. She'd done some research in the library, and she'd made an informal survey of the compound, mapping on paper where some tourist cabins could be built.

She'd painted a couple of bird portraits from her sketches at the mist nets, and then left the pictures in Max's study for him to see.

She'd also paid a visit to the village of Laguna Miguel, and she had some mixed results from her trip to share with Max.

Leaving no stone unturned, Julie had gotten input from the graduate students, having discovered that Max had told them about the plan to develop ecotourism at the research station. To her surprise, all four of them embraced the plan. They'd agreed that it was a basically good idea, one that had worked well at other facilities similar to Manu River.

Would tourists get in their way or impede their work? Julie had asked them. No, they'd told her. On the contrary, they would welcome being able to share their enthusiasm with interested visitors. Those visitors would then return home as ambassadors for the rain forest.

Noelle even suggested that the station launch a volunteer program, whereby people would pay to work at Manu River in exchange for room and board. Such a program would satisfy people's need to "give back" to the environment, plus it would bring in additional revenue. Julie praised Noelle for her idea and included it in her report.

As Julie waited on the dock, she reviewed everything in her mind. She'd run all the numbers and her financial projections were complete. She'd written a draft of her report for Pierson-Roth, and she was ready to make a final recommendation. All that remained was to tie up a few loose ends and her job at Manu River would be complete.

But, talk about loose ends. Julie might have a lot to say about Manu River's future, but what did she know for sure about her own future? Her relationship with Max was a big unknown.

He'd shown interest in her, but what were his ultimate intentions?

Julie did know this: Whenever she pictured returning to Washington State without Max, her heart sank. He had brought warmth and light into her life, and he had kindled a passion in Julie that took her breath away. He was the man she'd been yearning for. She was sure of that. A future without him seemed bleak beyond description.

But how did he feel about her? That was the big question.

Just as Julie was ready to abandon her vigil on the dock, she heard the sound of an engine. Straining her eyes, she looked downriver and watched as a boat came into view. In the boat were Cesar and Max, with Max at the helm. Her heart leapt with joy. Max was home.

Julie felt a mixture of unbearable excitement and suspense as the boat bearing Max pulled up to the dock. Max and Cesar disembarked and tied the boat to the landing. Then, after exchanging greetings with Julie, Cesar disappeared up the trail, leaving Max and Julie alone on the dock.

Time seemed to stand still for Julie as she and Max paused for a heartbeat or two and simply gazed into each other's eyes. Then Max smiled and said her name, closed the gap between them, and gathered her in his arms.

"Welcome home, Max," said Julie, hugging him with her cheek pressed to his chest.

The solid warmth of Max's body enveloped Julie like a balm. She felt so safe in his embrace, believing, as she did, that in his arms was right where she belonged. Reuniting with Max was a kind of homecoming for her, as well.

"God, I've missed you," said Max, kissing Julie's lips and temple. "Lima was one big, lonely city."

They kissed again, longer and with more intensity this time, drawing out the sweet sensation of their lips becoming reacquainted. The two weeks apart had been a very long time. The warm intensity of their embrace reminded Julie of a flower meadow blooming after a long, bleak winter.

"How was the conference?" asked Julie, as she and Max began walking up the path. Dusk was coming on.

"It went very well," said Max. He had one arm wrapped around Julie's waist and was carrying his duffel bag in the other. "How were things here?"

"Oh, the usual," she said, laughing.

Julie's heart was soaring with happiness. Not only was she overjoyed to see Max, but she had also come to realize, during his absence, that she'd formed a bond with both the rain forest and the research station. Manu River felt as comfortable and as welcoming as home to her now, as if she'd lived there for years. She would be sorry to leave.

"There was another crisis with the kitchen generator," she went on, catching Max up on the news. "Hernando fixed it, but he says he's now out of spare parts."

"Okay," said Max, nodding, "I'll order some tomorrow." He paused. "What else have I missed?"

"There was some excitement a couple of days ago."

"What happened?"

"Some monkeys made off with a bag of bananas that was accidentally left outside."

"Oh, yes," said Max, with an indulgent laugh, "bandit monkeys. I'm familiar with the species."

"Ted found a rare moth," said Julie, chattering on. "It doesn't even have a name yet."

"That must have made Moth Man happy," said Max.

"I'll say," said Julie. Then she added, "Oh, and we got a picture of a jaguar with the camera trap. That was thrilling."

"Ah, life in the rain forest," said Max, clearly glad to be back. "There's never a dull moment." He glanced at her. "What about your work here? Did you accomplish everything you wanted to while I was gone?"

"Pretty much," said Julie, nodding. "My report's almost finished."

"I guess that means you'll be leaving soon," said Max, in a thoughtful tone.

"I suppose," said Julie, keeping her voice neutral.

"Hmm."

"I've got so much to tell you," said Julie, shifting conversational gears as she and Max reached the clearing at the station. The clearing was deserted at the moment.

"I'm sure you do," said Max, his tone unreadable.

He set down his duffel bag and looked around at the quiet compound with a contented, proprietary air, like a sovereign surveying his kingdom.

As they stood there in the velvet dusk of evening, Julie wondered if Max had come to terms with the changes headed for Manu River. His time away from the station had certainly given him an opportunity to think things through and adjust his opinion.

When Julie glanced in Max's direction, however, she found nothing in his expression to reassure her that he'd accepted the inevitable. For all she knew, he was still clinging to his suggestion for a compromise, and stood ready to fight any plan to allow overnight visitors at the station.

Julie's heart squeezed with concern for Max. She feared that if he resisted long and hard enough, Pierson-Roth would either find a new director for Manu River or shut down the station altogether. Either outcome would mean a huge loss.

Julie knew that she had only a few more days in which to convince Max that mixing ecotourism with science had enormous potential. Of equal importance, she wanted him to understand that, however things turned out, she was on his side.

Just then, Max broke in on Julie's thoughts.

"Did you visit Laguna Miguel while I was gone?" he said.

"Yes."

"Well," he said, "what did you find out? Is your, um, mystery bird the real deal? Or is it as made-up as I thought it was?"

Julie hesitated. "The answer's kind of complicated," she said, with a little shrug.

"Hmm," said Max, raising one brow, "that tells me you didn't find it." He regarded her. "No surprise there. I'm tempted to say I told you so, but I'll spare you the indignity."

"That's big of you," said Julie, teasing him in return.

For a number of reasons, Julie thought it prudent to let Max assume what he liked for the moment. There'd be plenty of time later to go into the details about her trip to Laguna Miguel.

"Catch me up on the other stuff," said Max, changing the subject. "What's been going on at the tapir salt lick, for example?"

"I wouldn't know," said Julie. "I still haven't been out there."

"You haven't been to the tapir lick?" said Max, expressing surprise.

"Not yet," said Julie. "Noelle was going to take me there a couple of nights ago. But then at the last minute, we both decided we had too many other things to do."

"Well, we're going to have to fix that," said Max, with a decisive air. "You've got to see the tapir lick. It's an amazing place. I'll take you there myself."

"Okay."

"How about tonight?" said Max. "Could you be ready to go in, say, half an hour?"

"Sure, I guess so," said Julie. She regarded him. "But you just barely got back, Max. Don't you want some time to settle in?"

"That won't take long," he said. "Besides," he added, drawing her close, "I'd much rather have a date with you than unpack my duffel bag."

Julie laughed, infected by his enthusiasm. "What about dinner?" she asked. "Aren't you hungry?"

"I ate something on the boat," said Max. He glanced at his

watch. "While you're getting ready, I'll let everyone know I'm back, and then I'll grab a shower and some clean clothes."

"What should I bring?" said Julie.

"You'll need a flashlight," said Max, "and you should wear your boots. I'll take care of everything else."

"All right," said Julie, nodding.

"Oh, and Julie?" said Max.

"Yes?"

"Look," he began, in a sincere tone, "I know you're probably eager to talk to me about your report."

"Yes," said Julie, "I have so much to tell you. I have the final figures to show you, and I have something to tell you about tomorrow." She moistened her lips. "You see, while you were gone, I went ahead and—"

Max held up his hand and stopped her.

"Whatever it is," he said, "I'm guessing it can wait."

"I suppose," said Julie, privately relieved to put the subject off.

"I'm probably not going to like a lot of what you have to say," continued Max. He kissed her gently on the lips. "But may we agree to something?"

"Yes, of course, Max," said Julie, responding to the earnest look in his eyes.

"Let's agree," said Max, "to table that whole subject until tomorrow, shall we? Where I'm taking you tonight is a very special place. Let's not ruin the experience by locking horns over the Pierson-Roth plan."

He cupped her face in his hands.

"I've been away for two whole weeks," he added. "I've missed you so much, Julie. So what do you say?"

"It's a deal," said Julie, her heart reaching out to him. "We'll talk tomorrow."

"All right, then," said Max. He picked up his duffel bag. "I'll meet you in front of the lounge. The trail to the tapir lick takes off from there."

* * *

Thirty minutes later, Max and Julie began hiking into the rain forest. Max carried a pack and Julie wore her knapsack.

It was nearly dark by then. They walked in single file with Max in front, using their flashlights only in the areas where the shadows were the deepest. Following Max's example, Julie moved as quietly as possible and kept her conversation to a minimum, the better to soak up the atmosphere of the forest.

After walking half an hour or so, they arrived at some wooden steps leading up to a wide viewing platform, six feet off the ground. The platform had a roof and an open front.

It was dark by then. Julie quickly inspected the platform with her flashlight, noting the several mattresses lined up along the floor and a matching number of mosquito nets tied above them. Just then, she remembered something Max had once told her.

"Are we spending the night here?" she asked, turning to him.

"It all depends," said Max, setting down his pack. "Sometimes the tapirs show up early, sometimes later." He nodded toward the mattresses. "That's why those are here. When I first started bringing students out here to see the tapirs, some of them would fall asleep and miss everything." He chuckled. "Now, at least they can be comfortable."

"I want to stay awake," said Julie. "I hope Trixie will show up," she added, referring to the tapir whose picture she'd seen from the camera trap. "Do you think she will?"

"There's a good chance," said Max, rustling around in his pack. "And when she does," he continued, "I'll shine this and we'll get a good look at her." He held up a large flashlight with a red filter attached to the front.

"Why the red?" asked Julie.

"The light of a regular beam," explained Max, "would be too bright. It would frighten the animals, so we use a subdued red light instead. Tapirs don't seem to mind it."

"Where's the salt lick?" asked Julie.

"It's right there," said Max, shining his flashlight on the area directly in front of the platform.

Julie saw a shallow, muddy pond with dirt banks.

"I know you've already told me this," she said, "but why do the tapirs come here, again?"

"They come to wade in the pool," said Max, "and to eat some of the mud, for the minerals."

"I see."

"Parrots do the same thing," said Max. "There're a couple of parrot licks upriver, not far from here."

"Hmm," said Julie, her mind whirling with ideas. "You're lucky to have all these salt licks. They draw the birds and animals, which makes it easier to observe them."

"That's right."

"Tourists are going to love it here," said Julie, forgetting for a moment that she'd agreed not to bring up that topic.

"Oops, sorry," she added, and changed the subject. "So, how does this work? We sit here and wait for tapirs to show up, is that it?"

"That's the idea," said Max. "But in the meantime, I have a little something to share with you."

He reached into his pack and brought out a cloth bag.

Just then, Julie felt a mosquito buzzing around her face.

"Get away!" she said, and fanned the air with her hand.

"Time to take cover," said Max.

He untied a mosquito net hanging from the ceiling and lowered it over one of the mattresses. Then he and Julie removed their boots, crawled beneath the netting, and tucked the edges of the netting under the mattress.

"Okay, now we're safe from the mosquitoes," said Max, as he and Julie sat across from each other.

They remained still and silent for a few moments, allowing the darkened rain forest to work its magic. The air was balmy and lightly scented with night-blooming flowers. Frogs croaked in the reeds, and an open patch of sky above the pond was spangled with stars as crisp and bright as faceted gems.

Julie took a deep breath, feeling at one with her surroundings.

At that moment, with Max nearby, her world was complete and she wanted for nothing.

There was a rustling sound as Max pulled something from the cloth bag. It turned out to be a battery-operated votive candle, which he clicked on and then placed on the mattress. The votive gave the perfect amount of light, forming a little pool of illumination between him and Julie.

"This is like camping," said Julie, giggling at the sight of her and Max safely ensconced in the tentlike space, lit by the tiny flickering light. "I don't suppose you brought some trail snacks with you."

"Lima was fresh out of trail snacks," joked Max, as he again reached into the bag. "But I do have a couple of other things you might like." He smiled at her. "You couldn't go to Lima, so I've brought Lima to you."

"Oh, Max, you're so nice to me," said Julie, touched by his thoughtfulness.

Then she watched as Max popped open a can and poured fruit juice into two small glasses. He handed one of the glasses to Julie.

"Cheers," said Max, as they clinked their glasses together and then drank.

"Mmm, this is delicious," said Julie, as she rolled the complex flavor around on her tongue. The juice had an exotic sweet taste, balanced by a note of tartness. "I've never tasted anything like this," she added. "It's wonderful. What is it?"

"It's passion fruit," said Max, his eyes smiling at Julie over the rim of his glass.

How perfect, thought Julie, feeling a warm surge of attraction for Max rise from her belly to her chest. She'd read about passion fruit in several different contexts, including one that suggested intense emotion.

And it was certainly intense emotion that she was feeling at that moment.

She lowered her gaze and drank, hiding her eyes from Max. She couldn't help but wonder if he'd chosen the flavor at random.

Or had he known exactly what he was doing and what message he was sending by sharing juice with her made from a delectable fruit named "passion"?

Next, Max brought out a pink cardboard box tied with string.

"Open it," he said, pushing the box toward Julie.

Julie set her glass aside and untied the string, eager to see what other surprises lay in store.

"Oh, how beautiful," she said, folding back the lid and finding two oblong shapes nestled in a bed of pink tissue paper. "What kind of cookies are these?" she said, glancing over at Max.

"Chocolate-covered macaroons," said Max. "They're a specialty at a certain bakery I know of."

He set down his glass and selected one of the cookies.

"Allow me," he said, moving closer to Julie.

He raised the macaroon to her lips, an intimate gesture that tempted her to take a bite.

Julie broke off a piece of the cookie with her teeth and chewed. A mellow flavor of sugary almonds, coconut, and chocolate filled her mouth. She savored the morsel and then swallowed.

"This might be the best thing I've ever tasted," she said. Having Max feed her was an added pleasure, of course.

Max offered Julie another bite and then handed her what was left of the macaroon. He reached into the box and pulled out the other cookie for himself. Then they ate and drank in silence, except for an occasional soft swooning sound from Julie.

"I love a woman who moans over her food," said Max, grinning at Julie as he swallowed his last bite.

"That was amazing," said Julie, finishing her macaroon and her juice. She laughed as she licked the corner of her mouth with the tip of her tongue. "Do I have chocolate on my face?"

"Yes," said Max, "and on your fingers too." He moved over to sit beside her. "Let me," he said, his deep voice vibrating on the night air.

Then he raised first one and then the other of Julie's hands to his mouth and slowly, sweetly teasing her, removed the chocolate from her fingers with his tongue and lips.

Julie caught her breath, knowing for certain that she would not taste chocolate again without thinking of this extraordinary moment. Never before had her attention been so completely focused on the present. All of her senses were fine-tuned, and she gave in to her feelings, utterly and without question. A gust of yearning raced through her, sweeping her away, and her heart brimmed with love.

"And now your lips," murmured Max, his voice husky as he pulled her to him.

"Oh, Max," whispered Julie, as she twined her trusting arms around his neck.

Chapter Eleven

Julie stirred in her sleep, slowly awakening in the pale light of early morning. She lay still and quiet, allowing her senses to savor the moment. The forest surrounding the viewing platform shone green and glistening, the leaves still dripping from an earlier downpour. Birds called from the trees and flowers scented the air.

It was the dawning of a new day, mused Julie, and she couldn't have felt any happier. What a joy it was to awaken in the embrace of her sweet man. She and Max were lying nestled close to each other, sharing their warmth through their clothing. Their arms and legs were entwined, and their cheeks were touching. Sometime during the night, Max had pulled a blanket over the two of them, and now they lay snuggled together as one.

Max was still asleep. As Julie listened to his peaceful exhalations, his breath soft against her skin, she knew that she would remember spending the night in the rain forest with Max for the rest of her life. Her heart overflowed with love for him as she recalled his embraces and the tender endearments he'd whispered in her ear. Max was the friend and soul mate she'd been longing for.

With a little sigh, Max awoke. He nuzzled Julie's cheek and softly kissed her lips.

"Good morning," he murmured.

"Good morning, Max," said Julie, fitting the palm of her hand against the contour of his face.

They lay together for a while, caressing and talking quietly. Presently, they sat up and looked around.

"I wonder if Trixie was here during the night," said Julie, as she reached for her boots.

"We'll never know," said Max, with a smile.

Reading the amorous twinkle in Max's eye, Julie sensed what he was thinking. Even if a herd of tapirs had stampeded through the jungle the previous night, neither he nor she would've noticed, so intently focused had they been on each other, talking, kissing, and finally falling asleep in each other's arms.

As Julie and Max began their walk back to the research station, Julie's thoughts turned from pleasure to business. Her mind whirled with worrisome questions. What would Max say after he'd read her report for Pierson-Roth? Would he graciously bend to the inevitable? Or would he stubbornly cling to his position, thus putting his job and the future of Manu River on the line?

Julie also wondered how Max would react upon learning the details of her visit to Laguna Miguel. The mixed results of her trip were due to honest intentions and an unforeseen mishap. Julie hoped that Max would take those factors into consideration when he'd heard the whole story of her search for the mystery bird.

Perhaps most worrisome of all was the question of how Max would respond when he found out what was taking place at the research station that very day. Julie had set events into motion without either Max's knowledge or consent. He was sure to be upset when he discovered what she'd done. But she was counting on Max's good sense and his generosity of spirit to override his dismay, thus allowing him to see the wisdom in Julie's actions.

Julie mentally crossed her fingers, hoping all would turn out as planned. As she hiked through the forest with Max, however, she knew that the biggest difficulties still lay ahead. How she handled the next few hours would decide everything.

On a personal level, Julie's stomach twisted with apprehension. She was taking a huge gamble and she knew it. No matter how well intended her motives, if her plan backfired, Max would feel betrayed. He might never trust her again, and their fledgling romance would end. As she trudged through the forest, Julie's steps were as heavy as her anxious heart.

"What are those noises?" said Max, as he and Julie neared the research station. "It sounds like someone's driving stakes into the ground."

Julie held her breath and listened. Had the visitors gotten there ahead of schedule, and were they already setting up camp? She hadn't been expecting them until later that day, which would've given her time to share the news of their arrival with Max and let him get used to the idea. Now she groaned under her breath and braced herself for the worst. Her carefully laid plan was already going awry.

Julie and Max stepped into the clearing. Then Max halted in his tracks and stared across the open space to the opposite side. His eyes narrowed at the sight of a small group of people—eight or ten strangers dressed in the casual "jungle attire" of American ecotourists—who were setting up two-person tents. The sound of happy chatter and the hammering of rocks against metal tent stakes filled the air.

Pablo and another worker were helping out. Spotting Max and Julie on the other side of the clearing, the two men gave a cheerful wave and continued with their tasks.

Max swore under his breath and turned to Julie. "What's

going on?" he said, from between tight lips. "Who are these people, and what are they doing here?"

"I can explain everything," said Julie. "I wanted to tell you yesterday, but we agreed not to talk about—"

"Yes, all right," he said, cutting her off, "I remember. So tell me *now*, Julie. What's this all about?"

"Do you remember the deal we made?" said Julie. "Before you left for Lima, you agreed that I could invite a tour group here for a trial visit."

"But there was a condition," said Max, glowering at her. "You could bring people here *if* you proved the existence of that mystery antpitta."

"But I *can* prove it," said Julie, and then gave a helpless little shrug. "That is, I thought I could."

"What are you talking about?" said Max, sounding impatient.

"It's a real bird," said Julie. "I've seen it with my own eyes."

"Go on," said Max, but he sounded doubtful.

"When I went to Laguna Miguel," said Julie, "I spoke with several of the women who'd stitched a likeness of that bird into their embroidery. They swore it was real and they offered to show it to me."

"And?"

"They took me on a long hike in the forest," said Julie. "It was through difficult terrain, to the only spot where they've seen the bird. The location happens to be where the women collect a particular plant they use for dyeing cloth, so their find was really just a lucky accident."

Max nodded, listening.

"When we got to the spot," continued Julie, "the women imitated the call of the antpitta. After they'd whistled a couple of times, a bird hopped out of the brush and stood in the open for a few seconds. Before it could disappear again, I took a picture of it with my digital camera."

"Great," said Max, "show me the picture."

"Uh, this is where the story gets complicated," said Julie, moistening her lips.

"What do you mean?" said Max, frowning.

"I only got a quick look at the bird," said Julie. "Then I got so excited that my hands started shaking. So, um, the picture turned out kind of blurred."

"Show it to me anyway."

"I can't," said Julie, with an embarrassed shake of her head.

"Why not?"

"You know that bag of bananas I mentioned last night?" she said. "The one stolen by the monkeys?"

"Yes, what about it?"

"Well, those were my bananas," said Julie, "and my camera was also in that bag." She winced. "My camera's gone, Max."

He groaned and shook his head.

"But it's a real bird," said Julie, insisting on her find. "And it had a speckled band across the back."

"But you said you only got a quick look at it."

"Yes, but—"

"So maybe you just *think* you saw the speckling," said Max. "It could've been a trick of the light." He shrugged. "It happens all the time, even to the pros. In the right circumstances, a pigeon can look like a peregrine." He regarded her. "Did the speckling show up in the photo?"

"I don't remember," admitted Julie, trying to recall details from the blurred image.

"Well, did you show the picture to anyone else?"

"No, I was saving it for you."

He muttered under his breath.

"You don't believe me, do you?" she said.

"I believe you saw what you wanted to see," said Max. "You were so eager to prove me wrong that your eyes deceived you."

"What about the women who showed me the bird?" said Julie. "Are all of them mistaken too?"

"Not necessarily," said Max, shrugging. "What they showed you might not have been an antpitta. It could've been a spot-backed antbird, for example. That's a species with speckling across the back."

"But . . . but I was so sure," faltered Julie, suddenly feeling confused and out of her league.

"Well, never mind," said Max, dismissing the subject. "It would've been exciting to find a new species, but I knew it was a long shot."

He leveled his gaze at her and shifted gears.

"Now, what about these people?" he said, nodding toward the visitors and their colorful nylon tents. "I feel like we've been invaded, so please explain what's going on."

"After my trip to Laguna Miguel," said Julie, "I e-mailed a tour company in Cuzco. I asked if they'd be interested in sending a group of ecotourists to Manu River for a few days. The company jumped at the chance. If this first trip turns out as well as I think it will, the company in Cuzco can act as your permanent agent."

Max listened in silence.

"I explained," continued Julie, "that the tour members would have to bring their own food and tents, because Manu River isn't set up yet for tourism. I also agreed to show them around while they're here." She looked at him. "They won't be any trouble, Max. I promise."

"Yeah, right," said Max, his eyes dark with subdued anger. "You just went ahead and made all of these arrangements without even consulting me, didn't you?"

"Actually, "said Julie, "I'd planned to tell you about this in person, days before the group arrived, when you got back from Lima. Then your return was delayed, and by then, it was too late to cancel with the tour company. The group was already on its way."

"But we had a deal, Julie," said Max, shifting his weight.

"And I was sure that I'd kept my end of it," she said. "When

I contacted the agent in Cuzco, I had proof that the mystery bird existed."

"You didn't have any proof," he said, his tone hardening with accusation. "You saw a bird for a couple of seconds. You took a single, blurred picture. And then you carelessly let monkeys steal your camera." He glared at her. "That's not proof."

"I'll take you to the spot myself," said Julie, casting about for any idea that would make things right. "I'll show the bird to you. It's real, Max. I'm pretty sure it's an antpitta, and I think I saw speckling on its back."

"I'm sorry, Julie," said Max, "but 'pretty sure' and 'think I saw' just won't cut it."

Then Max shook his head, his body language telling Julie that he had no intention of chasing through the forest after a creature that was a figment of her imagination.

Without warning, tears welled up in Julie's eyes. She swallowed hard and spoke in a voice that shook with emotion.

"I was counting on you, Max," she said, tears spilling down her cheeks. She angrily swiped them away with the back of her hand. "I was counting on you to believe me. But even if I'm wrong, I'd still want you to understand that I was only trying to help."

He said nothing.

"I'll tell you what's at the heart of this," she continued, unleashing her pent-up frustration over his attitude. "It's your stubborn resistance to the changes, *inevitable* changes, Max, that are coming to this research station. You're a bright person and a wonderfully capable scientist—"

"Don't patronize me," he snapped.

"—but at the same time," she went on, ignoring his remark, "you are also the most pigheaded, intractable man I've ever met. Frankly, I'm beginning to wonder if you're worthy of this wonderful place. Maybe someone else should be in charge of this Garden of Eden, someone who can bend with the wind and see the benefits in creative change."

Julie paused to catch her breath before delivering her final volley. She knew that her next words might sever her personal connection with Max. But she recognized that nothing short of the blunt truth would suffice at that moment.

"You know what I think?" she said, looking him squarely in the eye. "It would serve you right to lose your position here. You don't deserve it."

With that, she turned on her heel and strode away from him.

Tears of anger, frustration, and crushed feelings coursed hotly down Julie's cheeks as she headed for her cabin. She'd said more than she'd meant to. But in her heart, she knew that Max had deserved her harsh rebuke. He *was* pigheaded and stubborn, and he was standing in the way of progress.

On balance, Julie was glad to have spoken her mind. And if the truth hurt, well, so be it.

The next couple of days passed in a blur of activity for Julie. She finished her report and dropped a copy of it off at Max's office, carefully timing her delivery for when she knew he wouldn't be there.

Still smarting from her last encounter with Max, Julie was avoiding him as much as he seemed to be likewise avoiding her. He took his meals at odd hours, she rarely saw him around camp, and they hadn't spoken since Julie's candid outburst.

Julie's heart squeezed with unbearable sadness whenever she reflected on how badly things had turned out between her and Max. The rift between them felt deep and unbridgeable to her, and it pained her to be anywhere near him. The sooner she left Manu River the better.

In the meantime, she spent the daylight hours with the tour group. She took them on hikes into the rain forest, introduced them to the graduate students, and explained the importance of the work being done at the research station.

It delighted Julie to observe the visitors' interest and enthusiasm, and she felt a sense of pride and accomplishment.

Through vision and hard work, she was helping to steer Manu River in a wonderful new direction. If Pierson-Roth accepted her recommendation—and Julie felt confident that they would—the research station would incorporate an element of ecotourism and would flourish for years to come.

Julie's only regret was that she'd failed to sway Max's opinion, and, in the bargain, had lost his affection. It broke her heart to imagine what might have been.

On the morning of the third day, Julie split the tour group in half, according to their interests. One half would accompany Noelle, who'd volunteered to take them out in search of an ant swarm. The other half would follow Julie along a trail for some basic art lessons. With Julie's help, her "students" would go home with sketches they'd made of plants and butterflies, wonderful personal mementoes of their adventure in the rain forest.

Julie watched as Noelle led her group into the jungle. The group included a woman and her eight-year-old son. The boy, clad in protective rubber boots, was almost dancing with excitement. Ants, little Joey had told Julie, were his "most favorite thing in the whole world."

Julie smiled to herself, recalling her own experience at a swarm of army ants. The eager little lad was about to see one of the most amazing nature spectacles on earth. She could hardly wait to hear his reaction.

Julie began handing out sketching materials to her group. Just then, she heard the sound of a boat arriving at the dock down by the river. A few minutes later, a man carrying a box emerged from the river trail and headed for the main building.

Assuming that the man was delivering the spare generator parts that Max had ordered, Julie turned back to the men and women in her party and gave some last-minute instructions. Then she led them along the boardwalk and into the forest.

* * *

"Max, what are you doing here?" said Julie, startled to see him walking toward her on the trail.

It was two or three hours later. Per Julie's plan, the two groups had rendezvoused a few minutes earlier. Noelle had then escorted everyone back to the research station for lunch, leaving Julie behind to finish a bird drawing she was working on.

"Noelle told me where to find you," said Max. He stopped in front of her. "Mind if I join you?"

Julie was sitting on a rock with her sketching pad on her lap. She looked up at Max and her heart squeezed with pain and yearning. The unexpected sight of him—dappled sunlight mantling his broad shoulders, eyes as blue as a macaw's feather—triggered an unbearable sense of loss in her soul. She looked down at her drawing, hiding the emotions that were welling up inside her.

"May I sit with you, Julie?" said Max, patiently waiting for an invitation.

Wordlessly, she moved over to make room. He sat beside her and glanced at her drawing.

"Very nice," he murmured. "Long-tailed woodcreeper. That's a handsome bird."

"Yes, it is," said Julie, filling in the beak with her pencil. "It's my last drawing here. I want it to be perfect."

"All of your drawings are perfect," said Max. "You're very talented."

Julie focused on her work, saying nothing.

"I found the two bird paintings you left in my office while I was in Lima," continued Max. "They're good enough to be in a field guide."

Julie remained bent over her sketching pad, determined not to let Max's unexpected appearance throw her off balance.

"I ran into Noelle and her group about an hour ago," said Max. "I helped them find an ant swarm."

"You *helped* them?" said Julie, glancing at him in disbelief.

"Yeah, I know," said Max, with a sheepish laugh. "Hanging out with tourists doesn't fit the image you've gotten of me, does it?" He paused. "But I have a confession to make. I enjoyed myself."

"I find that hard to imagine," said Julie, in dry understatement. She gave her drawing a final inspection and then put away her sketching pad and pencils.

"But it's true," said Max. "I had a great time. Those are very nice people." He chuckled. "I haven't seen that much enthusiasm in a long time."

"What did they think of the ant swarm?" said Julie.

"They loved it," said Max, "especially Joey, the little boy. Then, afterward, the most amazing thing happened."

"What?"

"Joey came up to me and said—" His voice caught and he stared into the forest.

"Go on," said Julie, noticing a hint of moisture in Max's eyes. "What did he say?"

"He said that when he grows up," said Max, clearing his throat, "he wants to be a wildlife biologist just like me."

There was a long, thoughtful pause. Julie was touched beyond words and her heart softened toward Max. She laid her hand on his arm, telling him through the language of physical contact that she understood how moved he'd been by the sincere declaration of an eager little boy.

"Take the credit, Max," she said. "You inspired someone today. Joey will grow up and become an advocate for the rain forest."

"Having that little boy say that to me was a humbling experience," said Max, and then he added with chagrin, "but not nearly as humbling as that lecture you gave me the other day."

"I'm sorry for some of the remarks I made," said Julie. "Honestly, I can't imagine a better director for Manu River than you. You deserve to be here more than anyone."

"Don't apologize," said Max. "I had it coming. I've been

a stubborn fool." He regarded Julie. "I read your report. It's brilliant, and I just want you to know that I support your recommendation. Ecotourism at Manu River will work. I'll *make* it work." He paused. "But I'll need some help."

Julie gazed into Max's eyes, hardly believing her ears. Was this the same man who'd fought her every step of the way?

"I'll need a manager," said Max, "someone to take care of the tourism end of things. I plan to ask Pierson-Roth to give you that job." He paused. "If you'll have it, that is."

Before Julie could respond, he went on, enthusiasm lighting his handsome face.

"I'm almost finished with my field guide," he said. "I'd be honored if you'd agree to paint the color plates."

The idea of teaming up with Max in this way had already occurred to Julie, when he'd first told her about his field guide. Now she could hardly believe that this secret wish of hers was within her reach.

Max continued. "You could work on the color plates here at Manu River," he said, "while we're building some cabins and expanding the dining hall."

"I-I hardly know what to say—"

"Just hear me out before you answer," said Max. "I know this is sudden, and I've given you plenty of reason to turn me down." He took her hand. "But I've had a change of heart, Julie."

"But you've been avoiding me," she said. "I naturally thought we were at a complete stalemate."

"I'm sorry to have given you that impression," said Max, gently brushing hair back from Julie's face. "But I thought you were avoiding me too."

"I was," she admitted.

"Truth is," said Max, "I needed some time to myself to digest your report and get my head straight." He gave a mysterious smile. "Plus, I've been busy looking for this."

With that, he pulled something from his pocket. He placed the object in her hand.

"My camera!" said Julie, gasping with surprise. "Where did you find it?"

"Actually, little Joey found it," said Max. "While we were at the ant swarm, his sharp eyes spotted a metallic glint on the ground. It turned out to be your camera."

"I was so sure that I'd never see it again," said Julie, shaking her head in disbelief.

"I've been looking for it everywhere," said Max. "I figured those monkeys would eventually tire of playing with it and drop it to the ground. So, for the last couple of days, I've been searching in their territory, hoping to find it." He shrugged. "I knew it was a long shot, but I had to try."

"Why would you spend so much time looking for my camera?" said Julie. "You'd already made it clear that you thought I was mistaken about the mystery bird."

"But I wanted to see the picture."

"Oh, I get it," said Julie, with a little sigh. "You wanted to prove how wrong I was."

"No, silly," said Max, with an affectionate smile. "I wanted to see the picture to prove how right you were."

"What?" said Julie. "I'm confused."

"I'll admit that I didn't believe you at first," he said. "You're not a scientist, and I was sure you were mistaken." He regarded her. "Then I realized that, in my smugness, I'd completely missed the point."

"What do you mean?"

"You may not be a scientist," he said, "but you're incredibly observant and have an artist's eye for detail. Your sketches and paintings prove that." He pressed her hand. "So, if you say that you saw an antpitta with speckling on its back, then that is what you saw, and I believe you."

He paused.

"It's taken every ounce of my willpower," he went on, chuckling, "to keep from looking at your picture. I haven't seen it yet, but may I please see it now?"

With trembling hands, Julie pressed some buttons on her digital camera and held her breath. The camera had been tossed about by monkeys and been exposed to the elements. Would it still work?

"There it is," she whispered, as the image of a bird appeared on the little screen. "It's blurred, remember," she added, quickly handing the camera to the expert.

Max studied the picture for a moment, not speaking. Then he slowly nodded and looked at Julie.

"It's an antpitta, all right," he said, "and it has speckling on the back."

"Are you sure?"

"I'm sure."

He pressed a button, zooming in on the image for a closer look.

"See here?" he said, pointing. "*That* is speckling."

"Oh, yes," she said, "I see it."

"This is a new species, Julie," he said, his eyes lighting up, "a brand new antpitta. And it's turned up just in time to be included in my field guide."

"You'll have to study this bird," she said, "and then give it a name."

"I've already thought of one," he said, smiling at her. "How about *Grallaria juliwinlockii?*"

"You'd name it after me?"

"Of course," said Max. "You followed your hunch and went looking for the bird. If it weren't for your persistence, the world of ornithology might never have learned of this exciting discovery. The women in Laguna Miguel led the way, but you delivered the proof. Good work, Julie."

"What an honor," she murmured. "I'm so excited, I don't know what to say."

There was an expectant pause.

"Well, you can start by saying yes," said Max. He leaned toward her, a vulnerable expression of hopeful expectation on his face. "How about it, Julie? Will you stay at Manu River and work with me? I need a tourism manager, and I can't think of anyone I'd rather have paint the color plates for my field guide than you."

Julie was speechless for a moment, her mind racing to keep up with so many exciting developments at once. But she knew what her response would be.

"Yes," she said, "I'll stay and I'll work with you, Max. I'd love to."

"Good, that's settled," he said, clearly pleased by her answer. "And now I just have one more question," he went on, his eyes revealing a depth of emotion. "But it's the most important one of all."

With that, he got down on one knee in front of Julie and took both of her hands in his.

"Darling Julie," he began. "Dear, sweet woman, I've loved you since the first time I saw you, and I've come to realize that I can't live without you. You're all I can think about, and I believe we're meant to be together."

He paused, adoring her with his gaze.

"If you will have me, sweet Julie," he continued, "I promise to love you with all my heart for the rest of my life. Will you marry me?"

With that, he reached into his pocket and withdrew a small box. He handed the box to Julie.

"Open it," he said, gently urging her.

Julie could hardly believe her eyes when she saw the ring that was inside the box. It was a golden band of interlocking vines and leaves, a design inspired by the rain forest and embellished with an inlay of lapis lazuli in the form of a blue butterfly.

"Oh, Max," breathed Julie, staring at the ring through a mist of happy tears, "this is the most beautiful thing I've ever seen."

"I'm glad you like it," said Max. "I hope it fits. I had it specially made for you in Lima."

He regarded her.

"That's actually why I was late getting back," he said. "I was waiting for the ring to be finished. In the end, I had to return without it, but I arranged for it to be delivered to the research station. I've been holding my breath, but it finally got here this morning."

Julie nodded, recalling the man who'd arrived by boat and then walked across the clearing with a box in his hands.

"And here I thought," she said, laughing through her tears, "that the man from the boat was delivering spare parts for the kitchen generator."

"He was sworn to secrecy," said Max, looking pleased, "just in case he ran into you before he found me." He smiled. "I wanted to surprise you."

"Well, you certainly have," said Julie, her voice trembling with emotion.

She held up the ring, admiring how the blue stones and the expertly wrought gold caught the mellow light of the surrounding rain forest, with its canopy of venerable trees arching above like a cathedral.

"This is lovely," she said. "The butterfly is absolutely perfect."

"On the day that we met," said Max, "you saw your first morpho butterflies, remember?"

Julie nodded.

"So it just seemed right," continued Max, "to create a ring that would always remind you of that day." He cupped her cheek with his hand. "I hope that day will always mean as much to you as it does to me."

Julie nodded again, feeling at a loss for words. Her heart had never felt as full of love and hope and tenderness as it did at that moment. Then, with Max looking on, she slipped the ring onto her engagement finger. It was a perfect fit.

"Dearest Max," she said, twining her arms around his neck, "you're the finest man I've ever known. I never dreamed I could be this happy. I love you with all my heart, and I want to spend the rest of my life with you." She gazed into his eyes. "Yes, I will marry you."

With a happy exclamation, Max rose to his feet, pulling Julie up with him. Then they entered each other's embrace, soul mates for life. Their kisses were long and sweet, sealing the bond of their love and commitment.

As Max held her in the strong, protective circle of his arms, Julie's heart soared with joy. She knew that, from that moment forward, Max would always be her champion, her friend and lover . . . her soft place to fall.